KU-289-240

Ryan's Legacy

Ryan Buchanan is given his father's pistol on the day of his eighteenth birthday, unaware of his legacy and the tragic events that lie ahead.

Ryan refuses to sell his land to his neighbour and is soon faced with a death sentence for killing a man even though he cannot remember the fight that witnesses say took place.

With his life in danger he uncovers secret details from the past that could cost him his life. . . .

Ryan's Legacy

Bill Williams

A Black Horse Western

ROBERT HALE · LONDON

ISBN 978-0-7090-9214-8

Robert Hale Limited
Clerkenwell House
Clerkenwell Green
London EC1R 0HT

www.halebooks.com

Typeset by
Derek Doyle & Associates, Shaw Heath
Printed and bound in Great Britain by
CPI Antony Rowe, Chippenham and Eastbourne

ONE

By the time the first ray of sunlight shone through the barn window, Ryan Buchanan had already been awake for nearly an hour, even though his Uncle Tom had worked him to exhaustion the day before. Ryan had hoped he would drift off to sleep before it would be time to get up to start his day's work, but he hadn't. He would be forever grateful to his dead pa's brother Tom and his Aunt Meg, and he was feeling guilty about telling them that he would soon be moving on.

Today was Ryan's eighteenth birthday. It was the day that he would receive the present that he had longed for ever since he had come to Uncle Tom's homestead almost five years ago; Ryan would be given the gun that had belonged to his late pa even though Ma, as he referred to his Aunt Meg, would be deeply troubled. Uncle Tom had also promised to tell him the details of how his pa was killed and would warn him about other things, but he had not even hinted what they were about.

Uncle Tom and Aunt Meg had become his adopted parents and he loved them as though they were his real ma and pa. He hoped that they would understand when the time came to tell them that he was leaving. They wouldn't want to stand in his way, but he knew that they would miss him.

Ryan started the day with his usual routine of a cold water wash over his upper body to remove the itchiness caused by the straw bed. Uncle Tom had planned to build an extra room on the small cabin, but Ryan had insisted on using the barn. He'd filled out a lot during the past year and had shot upwards as well and now towered over his uncle.

He'd been told that he got his thick blond hair from his ma, who had died in a tragic accident just before his pa had been laid to rest close to her in the town's cemetery.

Ryan opened the door to the cabin and was greeted by the smell of breakfast cooking and a chorus of 'happy birthday' greetings from Uncle Tom and Ma.

'I do believe that there'll be an extra man at the table today, Meg,' Tom said with a grin and then added, 'but I don't want you giving him a bigger portion than me just because it's his birthday.'

Meg stopped stirring the contents of the pan and hugged Ryan and hung onto him as the tears rolled down her cheeks.

'Will you look at that silly woman, crying on this man's birthday? This is a day for celebrating, not weeping. Here, let me shake this young man's hand.'

Meg released her grip on Ryan and wiped away the tears with the bottom of her apron and then smiled as her husband shook Ryan's hand.

'I tell you, son, you've got a grip just like your pa had. He had the same shovel hands that you've got and to think what a skinny little runt you were not too many years ago.' Tom paused and then added, 'That's enough of the chin-wagging. Go and open your presents over there.'

Ryan didn't really need to open the first parcel to know that it was the smart Stetson that he had been admiring in John Appleby's general store these past months. The thin flat parcel had him puzzled as he ripped open the wrapping to reveal a portrait of Tom and Meg.

'It's not really a proper present,' Meg said, 'but we expect that you'll leave here one day and perhaps it will help you remember us by. Old Judd Kenley did it for us while you were seeing to the herd one day. He was showing us some sketches he'd done while he was resting from setting his traps and it was Tom's idea that he should do the portrait.'

Ryan studied the portrait, which was a good likeness, and feelings of guilt swept over him. Maybe they had already sensed that he would soon be off to pastures new.

'Thanks, Ma. Thank you both and not just for these presents, but for everything that you've done for me. I guess I was born lucky to have kinfolk like you.'

Meg's eyes filled up again. Tom just smiled at his nephew even though he felt a lump in his throat, not helped by the reminder of the brother he had lost. He had carried doubts about keeping secrets from Ryan, including how his ma had actually died, which wasn't the way Ryan had been told. There were other secrets that

7

had been kept from Ryan, including things about his pa, but he would be told them today. Tom just hoped that he was right that Ryan had the strength of character to handle the revelations and that he would understand why they had been kept from him until now.

'Right, young feller, let's have our breakfast and then we have a busy day ahead of us, working up a thirst for our trip into town tonight. Then we can celebrate your birthday properly at The Thirsty Man saloon. I bet you're all fired up for tonight, son? Don't go getting too excited if the saloon girls start flattering you, because they do that to every man including the ugly and smelly ones.'

Meg gave her husband a disapproving look, but she was thinking that the girls wouldn't need to lie about Ryan's good looks and he was going to break some young girl's heart before long.

Ryan didn't want to disappoint his uncle by admitting that he wasn't looking forward to his first visit to a saloon. He'd seen men puking outside the saloon and others hardly able to stand up when he'd passed by. He still tried his best to sound enthusiastic in his reply and then he scanned the small cabin looking for the present he had been so looking forward to getting.

'Have you lost something, Ryan, or would it be this that you're looking for?' Tom asked and smiled as he reached under the table to retrieve the gun-belt and weapon that he'd hidden on the chair, handing it to Ryan.

Ryan took the shiny leather belt and holster and felt a mixture of emotions as he pulled the pearl-handled Colt from the holster and gripped it. The pistol felt so comfortable in his hand that it could have been custom made for him. Tom smiled at the excitement showing on his nephew's face.

Ryan realized that he was about to enter a man's world. He'd heard tales of men being 'called out' over the strangest things. Men had died because they had looked in the direction of a troublemaker, or spoken to a saloon girl that someone else had staked a claim on. Uncle Tom had told him how he would have to learn to walk away from trouble, but Ryan knew that wasn't going to be easy for him.

'Let's go outside. You can strap that belt on and we can fire a few shots off. It'll only be a few, mind, because my belly is longing for that bacon that Ma has prepared for us.'

Meg watched them leave and a worried frown appeared on her smooth and usually contented face. The calendar might show that Ryan was a man and there was no denying that he had the body of one, but to Meg he was a still a boy, her boy. She hated the idea of him wearing a gun and the dangers that it might bring him.

'Can't that wait until later?' Meg called after them, but they were too far away to hear. She sighed, knowing that from today she would have good cause to worry about Ryan's safety. She had always grieved for the mothers and wives who had lost their loved ones when lives had been taken by a bullet.

Tom had already strapped his gunbelt on and watched as Ryan fumbled with the heavy buckle on his belt.

'I guess your pa was a mite thicker round the waist than you when he last used that weapon, Ryan, but there

9

was no one more skilful with a gun than him. It just seemed to come natural and he wasn't one for doing much practising, but when he did you could have sold tickets to watch him and I'm not exaggerating.'

Tom was almost as excited as the birthday boy and was looking forward to teaching his nephew the rudiments of using a weapon. Not that he was anything special himself, not like his brother had been, but at least he was still alive and that meant he could get by. Tom was usually happy to walk away from trouble, which was something that his younger brother had never been able to do right from the time of his first fight with a much older boy.

'Now the first thing about using a gun, Ryan, is being able to stay loose. If you tighten up then you'll never be able to draw fast and that's a fact. Don't be too fancy either. Keep it simple.' Tom was thinking about the troubled look he'd seen on Meg's face when he added, 'There will always be someone out there looking for trouble, Ryan, but I hope you never have to use that weapon in anger and your pa would have wished the same thing.'

Tom didn't mind lying about his brother not wishing the weapon to be used in anger. It was likely that had he been here on this special day he would have been giving his son very different advice.

Ryan was disappointed when his uncle changed his mind about firing off a few rounds because he didn't want the cows to get spooked before they'd been milked. He told Ryan that there would be plenty of time for sharp shooting later.

Tom could see the look of disappointment on his

nephew's face and suggested that he did a few practice draws because he guessed he was just itching to handle the gun.

Ryan looked a mite sheepish before he spoke. 'It won't be the first time I've handled a gun, Uncle Tom and I've got a confession to make: this isn't my first gun.'

Tom smiled because he'd known all about Ryan's secret shooting sessions at the Briel Canyon that had started just after his last birthday.

'I didn't like being sneaky, Uncle Tom, but I just couldn't wait.'

'So that's why you reeked of gunpowder when you came home sometimes,' Tom said, pretending he didn't know about Ryan's not very well kept secret.

Meg watched her men folk ride off. There was a tear in her eye as she remembered seeing her husband and his brother set off for their weekly drink in town. Ryan was so much like his pa and Jack should have been here today and riding into town with his son and brother. She smiled when she recalled the happy times the two families had enjoyed before the double tragedy that had made Ryan an orphan.

'Happy days,' Meg sighed as she opened the door to the cabin, not knowing that she would soon be facing fresh misery.

TWO

They had stopped at the Briel Canyon so that Ryan could try out the gun he'd longed to hold and he impressed Tom with his sharp shooting. Tom had told his nephew that he might even be as good as his pa one day.

Tom was the more excited after they had headed out of the canyon and urged their mounts into a gallop in the direction of Carrsville and the saloon.

Carrsville had a population of 973, counting those that lived or worked on the ranches to the west of the town and it was expected to expand following the recent introduction of the railroad. Many of the early settlers had come at the end of the war with a mixture from both sides. Tensions had been high at first, but had now eased.

The town was proud of its fine church and small school built by the early settlers and that had helped to create a community spirit. The building projects had been organized by Thomas Carr, the town's first preacher. Following Carr's death the town council agreed to the popular suggestion that the town's name should be changed from Calshot to Carrsville in his honour. Until last year the town had boasted three saloons, but the town council had closed two of them following serious problems with gambling, brawling and a number of fatal shootings.

Tom's anticipation of the celebrations to come was accompanied by sadness, because it would be the first time he had been in the saloon since his brother and Ryan's pa and been killed there. He'd missed his weekly visits to the saloon after toiling on the ranch and perhaps after tonight he would start doing it again. Ryan would want to be with his younger buddies, but some of the original folks were still around. Those that had settled there had experienced hardship together and it had forged real friendships. Tom sometimes had regrets that if they hadn't refused Major Stratton's offer to purchase their land they would have moved away and then perhaps his brother would still be alive. Tom and Jack Buchanan had settled in adjoining ranches and the wealthy Major Stratton had longed to acquire them even though he had no use for the extra land.

Main Street seemed busier than usual even for a Saturday evening, and they steered their horses away from the two carriages that headed towards them. One of them was being driven by an attractive woman and Ryan copied his uncle's gesture of tipping his hat in her direction. The lady gave them a frosty look and Tom tilted his head up to illustrate that the lady was a bit snooty. Ryan figured that she must be a newcomer or perhaps a city lady on a visit, because townsfolk were usually friendly, even towards folks they hadn't been introduced to.

'I hope you ain't planning on taking that boy inside

that den of iniquity,' a voice called out from across the street. It was Marshal Keith Clancy and he was doing his best to appear serious and disapproving as he walked towards them.

'This ain't no boy, Marshal, and we aim to celebrate his birthday with more than a few cold beers and then one of Joey's specials at the diner before the floor show starts. I expect you're probably too old to remember your first drink, Marshal.'

The marshal smiled, but didn't reply to the quip as his eyes focused on Ryan's pistol which brought back some memories, including those that he didn't like being reminded of.

Marshal Clancy was an imposing figure at six foot three and barrel-chested. He had piercing blue eyes, a bushy beard, and showed that his front teeth were missing whenever he smiled, which wasn't often.

'I don't suppose it will be too long before this young feller spends a night in one of my cells if he is anything like his late pa and you, Tom Buchanan. No offence meant, Ryan. I had a lot of time for your pa. He was as straight as a die. He was also as tough as they come, but always a fair fighter. I was only kidding about your uncle because he's always had the good sense to be able to spot those who just want trouble. There are always plenty of those about, but you'll learn to pick them out with a bit of experience under your belt. I hope you enjoy your birthday, but don't get to like hard liquor too much because it will empty your pockets and likely bring you trouble.'

Marshal Clancy also had good reason to remember

the pistol that Ryan was carrying. It was the same pistol that Jack Buchanan had used when he saved the marshal's life after he was wounded during a bank robbery. One of the gang was about to fire another shot at the helpless marshal when Jack Buchanan shot and killed all three robbers.

Tom and Ryan tied their horses to the hitch rail and the marshal walked away down the sidewalk towards the diner, intending to fill his giant frame with some wholesome food. The marshal had never married and cooking wasn't a skill that he'd acquired, and he had no desire to while the diner served up his favourites. He also enjoyed his fair share of home cooking thanks to the kindness of a few spinster ladies and widows who delivered meals to his office. He had a particularly liking for Jenny Oldfield's apple pie which appeared on his desk every Sunday afternoon when he was on duty. The marshal's eyes always lit up when she pulled away the cloth covering the pie, but he never noticed the adoring look in Jenny's eyes or the sigh she often gave when she left his office after receiving no more than a few words of thanks.

Tom suggested that it might be a good idea if they called in at Appleby's Store before going into the saloon and purchase some boxes of shells so that Ryan could make lots of visits to the canyon to get used to his new gun.

John Appleby greeted them in his usual friendly manner. He didn't look seventy years old with his smooth, slightly pinkish skin and blue eyes that always seemed to be smiling. John planned to sell up this year mainly on account of his gammy leg. He'd tried using an assistant to do all the ferrying around the store, but it wasn't quite the same, and he thought it was time he did some serious fishing up at Lake Otwa. He planned to have a little cabin built on Main Street and sit and watch the world go by while he puffed on his favourite clay pipe.

Ryan cleared his throat and asked for two boxes of shells.

John sighed and shook his head, but held back the smile when he said, 'I know you make that big hunk of an uncle look like a midget, but you're too young for me to be serving ammunition.'

John had been selling Ryan shells for this past year and he laughed before he said, 'Happy birthday, young Ryan and you can have these on me.'

John reached under the counter and handed the two boxes of shells to Ryan and then related a story to him about the fancy gun he was wearing.

'A feller from back East who had more money than sense was in the store when your pa came in. He asked your pa if he could have a proper look at his pistol and then told your pa to name his price. Apparently the feller had a huge collection and he was something of an expert. He showed me a little pistol which he carried in a shoulder holster and said that one day it would be worth more than my shop and its entire stock. The gun was the only one of its kind and had been specially made for him.'

'I guess the man didn't want it badly enough,' said Ryan figuring that his pa had aimed the price too high.

'Oh, he wanted it and he would have paid for it, but

your dumb pa wasn't for selling. The city feller thought your pa was just trying to get him to pay more, but he finally left the store a very disappointed man. He'd handed your pa a card with his details on in case he ever changed his mind, but before he left the store your pa had torn the card up and left the pieces on my counter.'

Tom and Ryan were leaving when the storekeeper shouted after them that maybe they'd discovered gold on their land and didn't need the money. Ryan and Tom laughed at the thought as they made their way to Ryan's horse and put the shells in his saddle-bag.

Anyone entering the saloon for the first time would have thought there must have been a fire. The room was thick with smoke – most of the men were smoking a cheroot, or had a clay pipe in their mouth or hand. The piano player looked to be the oldest man in the saloon by at least two score years, but he was energetic enough as he thumped on the keys. One drunken cowboy had been pestering a saloon girl to dance with him, but he was having trouble standing up, until she gave him a shove that sent him sprawling to the floor, much to the amusement of those watching. The cowboy wasn't hurt, but seemed content to curl up and sleep off the effects of the drink, but two of his buddies dragged him across the floor and out into the street amidst more laughter.

'It's been a long time, Tom. Welcome back,' said Jonty the owner of the saloon and then surprised Tom when he said that Vicky had mentioned that Tom and Ryan would be celebrating Ryan's birthday tonight.

Tom introduced his nephew to Jonty who then declared, 'The first drink is on the house, but I can't promise that one of the girls will give you a free one, Ryan.'

'I don't think a good looking lad like Ryan will have any shortage of girls, Jonty and he won't need any money for that sort of thing when the time comes, but tonight is all about drinking and good male conversation.'

Tom and Jonty laughed and Ryan looked a little embarrassed because one of the girls had just looked his way and given him a big smile and a wink.

John Theodore Thomas had bought the saloon ten years ago after he'd been shot during an incident in a card game and decided to give up being a professional gambler. He couldn't remember who had given him the name Jonty, but it had stuck.

Tom's advice that Ryan should sip his beer slowly was wasted as Ryan gulped it down and placed the empty glass on the bar counter.

Tom told Ryan that he could see this birthday was going to cost him more than a few dollars, but it was a very special occasion and he had come prepared for it. He tapped his shirt pocket to signal that he had enough money.

Tom was ordering the second drink when Vicky, who was in charge of the saloon girls, sidled up to them and smiled.

'I've missed you, honey,' she said as she looked Ryan up and down.

Vicky kissed Ryan on the mouth and didn't appear to want to stop. Ryan gave Tom an innocent shrug and then replied, 'I've missed you too, honey.'

Tom was taken aback that Vicky knew Ryan, but he was

in for an even bigger shock when Ryan introduced Vicky as his girlfriend.

'Nice to meet you, Miss Vicky,' replied Tom as he shook Vicky's hand.

Victoria Armitage was thirty-three years old and had about the most shapely figure a man would wish to see and a cleavage that was always on show. The hips were wide and the waist trim, but it was her inviting hazel eyes and shoulder length blonde hair that also attracted men. Vicky had been widowed three times and hadn't mourned the last two, who had treated her badly, but she still managed to smile her way through life and she enjoyed the company of men.

'Vicky would like to meet Ma over at the ranch and I was wondering if Ma would mind it being this Sunday after Vicky has been to church. Do you think that would be all right, Uncle Tom?'

Tom was on the point of telling them it would be all right, but wondering what Meg would think of Vicky when Ryan laughed and nearly sprayed Tom with the beer he had had just sipped.

Ryan confessed that he had only met Vicky the other day when he'd helped her carry some parcels from the store. When he'd mentioned the plans for him to visit the saloon on his birthday Vicky had suggested playing a joke on his uncle.

The saloon was filled with the laughter of those who heard Ryan's confession about Vicky's joke. There was no indication that the mood would change before the evening was over and that blood would be spilled on the floor.

19

THREE

Meg Buchanan had been pleased that her Tom had kept his promise to stay in town for the night and not to try and bring home young Ryan in the dark, but she fully expected them to be home in time for breakfast. No doubt she would only hear an abridged version of what Ryan got up to on his first night in a saloon. Meg hoped he hadn't suffered like her young brother had all those years ago. Her brother would never forget the night his buddies roped him inside a water trough after his birthday celebrations. He was still there in the morning until he was untied by the marshal.

The last few years had been happy for Meg after experiencing more than her share of sorrow. Her younger sister Eileen had married Ryan's father Jack a year before she married her Tom. There had been many jokes about two sisters marrying two brothers and she often teased Tom that she had got the ugly one. Tom had never been as handsome as Jack, but she loved him dearly and their love had grown stronger as they had coped with the heartache of the three miscarriages that she'd suffered.

20

Eileen and Jack had settled in the small ranch next to theirs and Meg wondered if young Ryan would live there when he took himself a wife. She often talked to Ryan about his mom, and filled in some of the things he'd forgotten about her or hadn't had the chance to learn, such as what a wonderful and beautiful woman she'd been.

Meg wondered how long Ryan would stay with them now because she knew that he would want to be moving out soon and seeking a bit of adventure. Tom would miss him and not just because he was a hard worker. He was the son that she and Tom never had, although they had done their share of arguing when they disagreed over things on the ranch. Ryan's energy meant that he wanted to do everything in a hurry and sometimes got frustrated with Tom, who was a plodder. Tom needed to think carefully and plan everything before he started work on even the smallest of tasks. Meg was busy sweeping the wooden floor of the porch when she spotted the two riders in the distance. She hurried inside and placed the pan on the stove in preparation for making the coffee that she was sure that her menfolk would appreciate. Their mouths would be dry and young Ryan's head would likely be pounding.

When she returned to the porch she was carrying a rifle just in case it wasn't them. Visitors were rare and Tom had drilled into her the need to be on her guard whenever he and Ryan were away. There had been times when some homesteads had been attacked during the Civil War, but those troubles were long over.

Meg had not fired a rifle since the single lesson that Tom had given her. He had laughed when she had closed her eyes before pulling the trigger, but she had hit the target and did it again and again, proving that it was no fluke. The riders were closer now and she placed the gun against the porch railings when she thought she recognized them.

When Meg went to greet her menfolk she was soon troubled and puzzled when she saw the glint of the marshal's badge in the morning sunlight. They hadn't returned home together and the marshal's presence meant there must have been some trouble.

As Ryan dismounted and came towards her she could see his anxious face that also carried some guilt. He hugged her tightly, but was struggling to say the few brief words that he'd rehearsed. The marshal was tempted to tell her the bad news, but held back.

'Uncle Tom is dead, Ma, and I'm so sorry.' Ryan finally blurted out.

Meg struggled to take in the news and she eased Ryan from their embrace and looked at the marshal for an explanation.

'I'm sorry, Meg. Tom got into an argument with some of Stratton's cowhands and he was shot. Young Ryan feels guilty as hell for not joining in, but I've tried to tell him that he wasn't to blame. Tom shot one of the trouble-makers, but he only wounded him. They'd probably all had too much to drink and it just got out of hand.'

Meg's face showed no indication that the news had registered with her as she addressed the marshal in her usual quiet tone.

'Can I offer you some refreshment, Marshal, before you head back to town?'

She was still in a state of shock and behaving as though the news wasn't real when she calmly suggested that Ryan went inside and got himself cleaned up.

The marshal explained that he needed to be getting back to his office and then added, 'I expect you'll be coming into town later. Tom is laid to rest at Moses Carter's, but if there is anything I can do then I'll be just down the street in my office. The whole town will be devastated when the sad news gets out because you know how popular Tom was. It's no consolation, but I wouldn't be surprised if the town council calls for a ban on carrying arms after this. Although when they tried to impose it once before it was thrown out by some members.'

'Thank you, Marshal, you have always been a good friend to us. I best get inside and make sure that the boy is all right. It isn't fair that he should carry the burden for what has happened.'

When Marshal Clancy returned to town he sensed an unusual quietness and a subdued atmosphere. The town had seen its share of violence since he'd been appointed marshal ten years ago, but Tom's death was different because he'd never been a troublemaker. John Appleby was outside his store pinning up a 'closed' notice and he just gave the marshal a polite nod, which was unusual, because Appleby liked to chin-wag. Two of Meg's old friends were dressed in black and were heading for the town's church, no doubt to say a prayer, asking for Meg to be given the strength to cope with her loss.

The marshal guided his dapple gray mare to the hitch rail outside his office and tethered it next to a familiar horse. Its owner was probably waiting to see him, but the marshal needed to take care of something first and headed along the sidewalk to Moses Carter's funeral parlour.

Moses was busy putting some fittings on a coffin and he looked stressed, but his face brightened when he recognized the marshal, anticipating that he was about to bring some more business his way.

'I thought you might want to know, Moses, that Meg Buchanan will be in town shortly and will want to see her Tom. I hope you'll keep your bill down because Tom barely eked a living out of his ranch business.'

'That won't be a problem, Marshal. We've just put Tom in this fancy coffin and he's looking very presentable seeing as neither of those two bullets hit him in the face. Mrs Buchanan needn't worry about paying for anything.'

'That's very generous of you, Moses, and I'm sure that she'll appreciate it.'

Moses looked as though he'd been insulted by the suggestion that he would offer charity to any of his customers. Moses was the thriftiest man in Carrsville and it was something he was proud of. Despite being one of the richest men in town he would never buy anything at the asking price. Moses may have inherited his bartering skills from his father who had been an Arab. His father had run a carpet and rug business in the city where Moses had grown up and had expected Moses to take it over, but Moses had other plans; he had figured that there was more profit in burying people and business would always be good in a violent country where people carried arms and drank hard liquor.

'Yes, Major Stratton is a very generous man, as I told him when he was here earlier. I think he was planning on seeing you while he was in town, Marshal.'

The marshal looked troubled and declined Moses's invitation to look at Tom Buchanan. He had a good idea what the major wanted to see him about and the act of generosity by one of the wealthiest cattle barons in the territory usually had a motive behind it.

Major Stratton's well bred black stallion seemed to be objecting to the marshal's horse tethered alongside and was edging away from it when the marshal passed by and entered his office. Stratton was talking to Deputy Bob Collins and the deputy seemed relieved to see the marshal. Stratton had a reputation for being fiercely loyal to those that worked for him and the marshal guessed that the major was here to plead for Cal Rawlins who was being held in one of his cells. If the marshal was expecting a hard time from the major or having to listen to lots of persuading that Rawlins was a good man then he was in for a surprise.

'Good to see you, Marshal. I was just telling your deputy that if my man Rawlins didn't kill Tom Buchanan in self defence then I hope he hangs and it serves as an example that this town will not abide wanton killings. Buchanan was a decent man and a fine neighbour of mine, not to mention a hard worker and a highly respected member of our community.'

Major Stratton was sixty-two years old and young looking for his age. His thick dark hair was cut by the town's barber every Tuesday and his former aide from his army days trimmed his handlebar moustache every morning. His brown eyes were often probing and, as expected for someone with a military background, he was a strict disciplinarian. His father had been a general and Stratton had been disappointed to have left the army with such a low rank, but he hadn't made friends in high places with his brusque manner. Stratton had also been a very poor leader of men and a failure when it came to planning tactics and had lost many brave soldiers as a result of his incompetence on the battlefield. His arrogance had prevented him from acknowledging his many failures, but he had excelled in business and established an empire built on the inheritance he had received following his father's death.

Marshal Clancy was remembering that Tom Buchanan had never been one of the major's favourite people since he'd repeatedly refused to sell him the Buchanan land. Perhaps the major had been reading the marshal's thoughts and seen his expression of doubt.

'Buchanan and I had our share of disagreements and I was surprised and disappointed that he turned down my very generous offer to buy his land, but he had principles and I admire that in a man. So, what's going to happen to Rawlins, Marshal?

Before the marshal could answer the major told him that whatever was decided the marshal would have his full support.

'According to everyone I've spoken to it was Tom who drew his gun first and he did wound your man, Macey. Rawlins was doing a lot of bad mouthing, which might have been the cause of the trouble starting, but I'm going to release Rawlins. I'll be making sure that he understands that if I hear that he's goaded someone else like he did Tom then I'll let a jury decide next time.'

Stratton hid his satisfaction with the way things had gone when he replied, 'Well I think you've just shown us what an experienced lawman you are, Marshal, and you need have no fear of Rawlins stepping out of line again. I'll make sure of that. I'll bid you good day then, Marshal, and I expect I'll see you at the funeral tomorrow.'

The door had barely closed when the marshal shook his head and said to his deputy, 'He's a smooth talking, smug bastard. I would love to have been able to send Rawlins to trial, but Stratton would have done everything he could to get him off.'

'He seems all right to me. He was telling me that he's paying for Tom's funeral,' said the greenhorn deputy.

'Take it from me, Stratton doesn't give a damn about Meg Buchanan and that gesture is just for show. Men like Stratton always have a motive and you'll learn that in time. We'll let Rawlins stew in his cell until Meg and Ryan Buchanan have been to see Tom and left town. I wouldn't want Ryan bumping into him.'

FOUR

Ryan had expected that Ma would have wanted to get to town as soon as possible, but she had insisted that there were things that needed to be attended to around the homestead and animals to be fed. She seemed more concerned about him than herself and hadn't even cried yet, which puzzled him. He could only guess that people became hardened to bad news when they had experienced so much of it. The marshal had let him sleep in his house after his uncle had been carried away from the saloon and he'd tried to give him some advice, which he'd repeated on the ride home that morning.

Ryan had been bedridden with a serious bout of fever when his ma and pa had been buried, so attending a funeral was going to be a new experience for him, but he would be strong for Ma.

Ma gathered some clothes and told Ryan to wear his Sunday best suit. She was wearing a black dress with a matching shawl pulled over her shoulders. She fussed over his tie not being straight and brushed his coat with her hand. He would normally have shown his objection, but not today. He still wished that she would show some emotion because he knew that she wasn't a hard natured lady, despite her experiences of past grief. He had been on the verge of crying himself a number of times, but he had held it back, believing that it wasn't proper for men to show their emotions. If he did cry at some point it would be where no one could see or hear him.

Even the dog was subdued as it watched the cart trundle away, sensing that something was wrong as he remained on the porch instead of escorting them off the property, barking his disapproval at being left behind.

The first part of the journey to town had been made mostly in silence, but then Meg started reminiscing and telling Ryan about how she first met his uncle and how they had struggled. She told him other things that he'd never heard about before, including the babies she'd lost and how her father had been found dead in the snow when he'd tried to get help when her mother was ill. The help would have arrived too late and Meg and her sister had been left to fend for themselves after they had lost both parents during the most severe winter that anyone could remember.

As they entered Main Street they felt the subdued atmosphere just like the marshal had earlier; the town was showing its respect today for one of their own. The saloon had a 'closed' notice pinned to one of the wooden supports at the entrance. Some thirsty cowboys would be in for a disappointment, especially those who had ridden some distance, anticipating a cold beer or having a saloon girl for company.

Appleby's General Store had a more presentable notice than the saloons and it said: 'Closed Until Further Notice' that Ryan guessed would be when the funeral was over.

Moses Carter was probably most folk's idea of an undertaker, being tall and thin faced with a long nose and an expression that would likely frighten most children and even some animals. Moses had been looking out of his office window and he hurried outside and helped Meg down from the cart before offering his condolences to her and Ryan and then directing them inside the funeral parlour.

'I'll leave you with your loved one, but perhaps you might wish to know that Major Stratton has kindly agreed to cover the costs of all the funeral expenses as well as a little reception at the church hall.' Moses had been rubbing his hands as he'd spoken as though to keep them warm, but it was a habit he had of doing even on the warmest of days. He bowed and retreated from them and disappeared into his back office to prepare the bill he would be handing to Major Stratton after tomorrow's funeral.

Meg was too busy staring inside the coffin at her husband to have taken in what the undertaker had said. Ryan had held back, but stepped forward when invited to by Meg and put his arm around her. He had never seen a dead body prepared for burial before. He was surprised at the peaceful expression on the face of his uncle that had been screwed up in pain the last time he had seen him. Ryan was drawn to the hands that usually bore the marks of his uncle's manual labour, but they had been

30

scrubbed and now they looked pale and slightly strange. The fingernails had never looked so clean despite Meg's scolding and insistence that her men washed their hands before they sat down for their meals.

'Tom, what have they done to you, my love?' Meg said with a smile on her face caused by the sight of the silk shirt and then added, 'Could you ever imagine seeing your uncle in such a frilly shirt, Ryan? He's a proper dandy, but I shan't complain because he looks so peaceful and even handsome. See, I've said it, Tom. You really do look handsome. Don't you think so, Ryan?'

Meg had looked towards the ceiling as though Tom was listening to her and she'd been smiling as she'd spoken.

Ryan dodged the question when he answered, 'He does looks so peaceful, Ma.'

Ryan didn't quite understand at first what Ma meant when she asked him if he would leave her for a moment to say her goodbyes to his uncle and when he did, he felt awkward and quickly walked towards the door.

Ryan sat on the sidewalk and, looking across the street, saw the outside of the saloon being cleaned by one of the bar staff. He was thinking that the place should be burned down. How could it be that a man could be laughing and enjoying life and within minutes be lying on the floor taking his last breath and his blood spilling on to the floor? Ma had told him that she knew of friends who had been beaten by their husbands as the result of drinking and who had gambled away their homes because of their habit. Maybe some of those ladies who had marched through Main Street last year carrying

31

banners and calling for the devil's drink to be banned might not have been crazy after all.

He realized now that perhaps Ma had been trying to warn him that liquor could ruin people's lives and it had certainly devastated theirs. The marshal had told him that drink in moderation wouldn't harm anyone and for some it helped them cope through difficult times and take their mind off what was troubling them. The marshal had warned Ryan to avoid getting into a fight when he'd been drinking and also not to make a woman any promises he might regret in the morning.

Ryan turned his head away to rid his thoughts of the saloon and he saw the marshal approaching, He was grim faced.

'I just wanted you to know, son, that once you and Meg have left town I will have to release Rawlins.'

'How can that be, Marshal? He shot my uncle. I was there and so were lots of witnesses,' Ryan pleaded because the thought of Rawlins getting off scot-free only made things worse.

'I'm sorry, Ryan, but those witnesses would say in court that Tom drew first and Rawlins' attorney would claim his client acted in self defence. Do you want me to tell Meg?'

Ryan told the marshal that he would tell her and the marshal could see that his staying might make the young feller argue and get more upset, so he bid him farewell and headed back to his office.

Ryan was thinking that if the law couldn't provide justice then there was something wrong. He couldn't bear the thought that his uncle's killer wouldn't be made to pay for what he'd done. Anyone could have seen that Uncle Tom was affected by the drink, the way he was swaying and unsteady on his feet and it just wasn't a fair fight. Ryan had been brought up to respect the law, but now his mind was full of doubts about it providing real justice. Perhaps he would have to deliver it himself.

FIVE

Carrsville had the unusual distinction of having two cemeteries with one being reserved for the soldiers who had fought in the Civil War and those who had died after the war had ended. Some of those who qualified to be buried in the military cemetery were buried in the civilian cemetery if it was the wish of their families. Tom and Jack had served in the war, but it had been decided to bury Jack Buchanan near his wife Eileen.

Meg had thought it was fitting that her Tom should be buried close to his brother. She had told Ryan that when the day came she would also like to be laid to rest near Tom and her sister. The request hadn't helped Ryan's mood as he entered the cemetery. He still hadn't come to terms that he would never ever work alongside the uncle he had idolized. There would be no more teasing and banter and the finality of death had been difficult for him to take in. Now the surroundings and the occasion were helping him to finally accept that, sadly, it was all very real.

*

The effect of the solemn occasion was evident on some of the faces of those gathered around the freshly dug grave. Some had tears in their eyes, not just for the loss of Tom, but for the memory of their own loved ones who had been laid to rest nearby. Nearly a third of the graves were the final resting place of young children who had died from fever or some other infectious disease that their young bodies had been unable to fight off.

Ryan had seen the familiar figure of Rose Kelly who was attending the nearby graves of her three children and husband who had been trampled to death by a stampeding buffalo herd. The family had been on the way back from a picnic near their home and Rose had miraculously escaped serious injury, but often wished that she hadn't survived.

There was no holding back the tears today and they rolled down Meg's face when the minister, Abe Newton, paid tribute to a hard working and respected member of the community. The minister had ranted inside the church just a short time earlier about the dangers of arms and the effect of the demon drink that turned placid and God-fearing men into servants of the Devil. Now he only praised the memory of Thomas Lionel Buchanan.

Ryan felt his ma tremble beside him as his uncle's coffin was lowered into the grave and for a moment he thought she was about to throw herself on top of it. Ryan scanned the stern faces of the men gathered around and some gave him a brief nod while others lowered their eyes. He didn't sense any sign that their looks carried any accusation against him, but it didn't ease his guilt. He hoped that one day soon the body of Rawlins would be lowered into a grave where it belonged. Major Stratton had sent Meg a note of condolences and said that although some of his men had wanted to attend the funeral, he had forbidden it, not wishing to risk upsetting her. She had not been convinced of the major's sincerity and had barely finished reading the note before she had thrown it aside.

The gathering at the church hall was agonizing for Ryan as people had expressed their sorrow. Ryan questioned the sincerity of a few who seemed too eager to heap praise on a man they hardly knew. Ma had warned him that some people appeared to enjoy such gatherings and never missed a funeral service and it was like a pastime or a hobby to some. Ryan thought it was disrespectful because bereavement was personal. Some had just been passing through the town and had no connection with the family and he was on the point of telling them to leave, but held his temper in check. He was glad when it was time to leave and he turned down the marshal's suggestion that he join him for a drink in the saloon that was being opened just for close friends of his Uncle Tom. He knew that the marshal was well meaning, but Ryan wasn't ready to step inside the saloon that had such unpleasant and painful memories for him and told the marshal he needed to take Ma home.

Ryan had learned a lot about looking after the cattle and attending to jobs on the ranch, mainly because his uncle had allowed him to gain experience by his mistakes. He still wasn't sure that he could manage on his own or that they could afford to hire some help when needed. One thing was certain and that was he wouldn't be leaving as he'd planned while Ma needed to be comforted and supported. Ma was the most important thing in his life, but he knew that he couldn't just let what happened to his uncle pass. He had already decided exactly what he would do.

SIX

Six weeks had passed since his uncle's death when Ryan strapped on his pa's gun and rode out to the canyon and started his practice. His first shots missed the target because of his pent-up anger and he stopped because he was just wasting his ammunition. He holstered the gun and slumped to the ground and then sat with his back to the rocks and relived the moment in his mind that had ended with him cradling his dying uncle on the saloon floor. The thing that had haunted him most was the memory of his uncle's face as he looked at Ryan's, just before the first bullet had thudded into his chest. Ryan would never know if he was looking towards him, expecting his help, or was it a protective and warning look for him to stay out of trouble!

The marshal and Ma had tried to make him feel better, but he doubted if he ever would be until he did something to help him regain his own self respect. Perhaps there could be a second chance for cowards and that's what he believed he was because he had just frozen when he should have drawn his pistol. Even when his uncle had lain on the saloon floor gasping for his last breath and then closed his eyes, Ryan had done nothing. Why hadn't he pounded the life out of the man who had taken his uncle from them. He still didn't know what the argument had been about because he had drifted over to the other side of the saloon to talk to Janet, the youngest of the saloon girls. It had all happened so quickly and he had been taken by surprise, but there could be no excuse for not doing something. He knew that what happened would likely haunt him for the rest of his life.

He'd discussed with Ma what they would do about the ranch because managing the small herd required two men to drive the cattle to market, but John Scully, who was their closest neighbour, had offered to help.

Ma seemed to be coping with their loss, but she had seen her share of tragedy and not just the loss of her miscarried babies and both her parents. Ma had been one of nine children and all but one of her seven brothers never came back from the war and she'd never heard from the one who had deserted. Perhaps the worst tragedy of all was the loss of her sister, Ryan's mother, Eileen. Ryan had come to realize that womenfolk often show a toughness that matched the men who had coped with adversity when they had travelled out West to start a new life.

Despite Ma's determination to get on with her life after her loss, Ryan was reluctant to leave her alone for long and had resisted her attempts to encourage him to go and see some of his buddies. He had confined himself to his daily short trips to inspect the herd and visits to the canyon for his shooting practice.

*

Ryan was returning from his regular trip to the canyon when he saw a young woman leading a palomino horse that was obviously lame. He knew most of the girls from the town, apart from the saloon girls, but he had never seen this one before. Her blonde hair nestled on her shoulders and, as he got closer to her, he saw the palest blue eyes that he had ever seen. He figured she must be about his age and he noted how shapely she was in her expensive and tight-fitting riding outfit. He asked what the problem was, which he immediately regretted, because it sounded dumb. She looked cross when she replied, 'This silly horse has gone lame on me.'

Ryan smiled and said, 'I don't expect it did it on purpose.'

She returned his smile, 'It was probably my fault for taking her too close to the canyon and over the rough ground and amongst those loose stones.'

Her smile made him see a different person to the hoity miss of a few minutes ago and he slid down from his saddle and told her he would like to take a look at the horse.

'If you would be so kind,' she replied and he smiled again at her formality.

The mare didn't take too kindly to Ryan lifting its leg to inspect the hoof and bared her large teeth as she took a snap at him, but he managed to dodge clear.

'Easy does it, girl! I'll try not to hurt you, but that stone's got to come out,' he said trying to calm and comfort the animal.

Ryan gently lowered the horse's leg to the ground, unbuckled one of his saddle-bags and ferreted inside, pulling out a small knife.

The mare didn't object when he lifted the leg again, but started snorting and twitching when he gently loosened the sharp stone with his knife. There was a final snort, a shake of the head and it swished its pure white tail when the stone was prised free. Ryan held the stone in the palm of his hand as he showed it to the young woman.

'She might still feel a bit sore, but just try walking her around slowly and see how she feels before you try to ride her. She'll soon let you know if she objects because the wound is still causing her some pain.'

The horse was soon walking normally after it had covered the few small circles guided by its mistress, who was looking more relaxed and didn't seem bothered by the obvious attention Ryan was showing her.

'I expect someone would have come looking for me, but I am very grateful to you,' the woman replied after she had mounted the horse and prepared to ride off.

'I've never see you around before,' Ryan said, disappointed that she seemed in a hurry.

'I only arrived yesterday to stay with relatives. I'm from Clayton near Fulton City, but I don't suppose you have heard of it. Thank you for your help. You are a knight in shining armour.'

'Perhaps I know your relatives,' Ryan suggested, eager to keep her talking.

'I wouldn't think so,' she replied and bid him farewell. She heeled her horse into action, leaving Ryan disappointed that she hadn't stayed longer.

SEVEN

Ryan had pulled his sorrel up to walking pace as he entered Main Street. He had chosen tonight because he knew the saloon would be busy, just like it had been on the fateful night of his birthday. The man who had killed his uncle might not be there, but tonight wasn't just about revenge; it was also about Ryan facing his demons.

There was no room on the hitch rail outside the saloon and some of horses bunched together carried the Stratton brand. Ryan steered his horse across the street to the hitch rail outside the undertaker's and that brought back more unpleasant memories. He secured his horse, took a deep breath and crossed the street, pausing for a moment before he pushed open the swing doors to the saloon.

The smoked-filled bar was noisier than last time and if he expected it to become silent and all eyes focus on him he would have been mistaken. The first eyes to look his way and stayed locked on his were those of Susan, the new saloon girl. She looked disappointed when he ignored her and headed towards the one vacant spot at the bar. He didn't see a man at the table nod to draw his attention to his buddies.

'What'll be, young feller?' asked the barman, who Ryan hadn't seen before. There was no sign of Jonty, the saloon owner.

Ryan ordered a beer and while he waited for it to be served he scanned the saloon, spotting a few familiar faces. Joey Mason raised a hand, while Doc Norris nodded and gave him a sympathetic look. As usual the doc had a glass of sarsaparilla in front him while he sat at one of the gambling tables.

Ryan finished his third beer and was thinking about moving on, partly because of the piano player struggling with an out of tune piano. A saloon girl who was singing in sympathy with the piano didn't help, but his plans to leave were about to be halted.

'Do you think that gun he's wearing is loaded, or is it just for show?' Paul Bryce scoffed and then laughed along with his two buddies from the Stratton ranch who were sat near the bar.

'Perhaps he doesn't like loud bangs,' Bryce scoffed again and then added, 'I'm surprised the chicken-livered coward who didn't help his uncle would dare show his face in here. I bet his old man had a yeller streak down his back as well.'

Ryan whirled around and dragged Bryce out of his chair and then delivered three fierce blows to Bryce's face that sent him sprawling to the floor. Bryce struggled to stand up and when he finally did his hand reached towards his holstered Colt .45, but he was pistol-whipped

43

in the face by Ryan who had drawn his pistol with light-ning speed. Joey Beale made a move towards Ryan, but was met with a flurry of blows before he fell alongside Bryce on the saloon floor.

'Don't move,' Ryan ordered Bryce's other shocked buddy who was still sitting down and hadn't planned to go to the aid of his battered friends. Beale was out cold, but a dazed Bryce had sat up and didn't understand Ryan when he first ordered him to open his mouth.

'I said open your mouth or I'll smash those teeth of yours and you'll be as gummy as a grandpa,' Ryan snarled into Bryce's bloodied face.

Bryce opened his mouth and the blood from his broken nose trickled over his lips and then onto the barrel of Ryan's pistol whose tip had been forced into Bryce's mouth.'

'Jesus, he's going to blow his brains out,' shouted one of the men standing near the bar.

Ryan froze when he heard the unmistakable sound of a pistol's hammer being drawn back and then he slowly turned his head towards the direction it had come from. He hadn't noticed the man when he'd scanned the bar earlier and now he heard his calm voice say, 'You're not thinking of your ma, boy.'

Ryan's anger eased at the mention of the woman who meant so much to him.

The marshal held out his free hand and Ryan slowly removed the pistol from Bryce's mouth and handed it to him. Marshal Clancy used his own pistol to point towards the saloon door and Ryan started walking. As they left the saloon the piano playing started up and things inside the saloon were almost back to normal before they had reached the marshal's office across the street.

'Lock Ryan up, Deputy, and I'll come and have a word with him,' ordered the marshal and he locked away Ryan's pistol in a small cupboard next to the rifle rack on the wall behind his desk.

Deputy Ty Milligan had known Ryan from the time they'd gone fishing together with Ty's pa and Ryan's Uncle Tom and he felt awkward as he escorted Ryan to his cell.

'What have you been up to, Ryan?' he asked. He knew it was something bad because the marshal had looked so serious, but he wasn't expecting the reply he got.

'I nearly killed a man, Ty, and he wouldn't have deserved it.'

'You're kidding, me?' questioned the shocked deputy.

'No, he isn't,' said the marshal as he appeared behind his deputy and then added, 'Go and brew some coffee, Ty, while I have a word with this young fool who needs to curb his temper.'

Ryan appeared sheepish when the marshal gave him a disapproving look while shaking his head, but he didn't speak to Ryan until his deputy had closed the door that linked the area of the cells to the main office.

'Would you have pulled the trigger and splattered what little brains Bryce has around the saloon?' the marshal asked while keeping his eyes fixed on Ryan's.

'I honestly don't know, Marshal, but if you push me for an answer then I think it would be a yes and it scares me.'

'And you disappoint me, Ryan, that you would let Meg down after all she's been through. I know you're still feeling guilty because you didn't help your uncle, but killing Bryce wouldn't have solved anything. You were lucky tonight that you didn't pull that trigger.'

'I don't feel lucky, Marshal,' Ryan replied knowing how close he had come to ruining his own life as well as Ma's.

'Just supposing you had drawn your pistol that night, what do think would have happened?' asked the marshal, but he didn't give Ryan a chance to answer before he continued, 'Well, I'll tell you. Tom would probably have still been killed, and you might have avenged him there and then, but now you'd be dead after swinging from the end of a rope. Just like you would have done if you had killed Bryce tonight and what do you think that would have done to Meg?'

Ryan was feeling as guilty as hell after the marshal had hammered home the effect his actions would have had on Ma.

'What's going to happen to me, Marshal?'

'I don't know. What you threatened to do was just as about as serious as it can be short of killing someone. You might have to go before a judge, unless you can convince me that you are going to sort yourself out. I'll sleep on it and let you know in the morning what I've decided to do. Perhaps you need to get a sweetheart and get on with your life. You can't bring back your uncle, Ryan, and I'm telling you for the last time that you shouldn't blame yourself for what happened to him.'

The marshal left a troubled Ryan to do some serious

thinking. He didn't regret tackling Bryce who had been spoiling for trouble, but the marshal was right about lots of the things he'd said.

Ryan hadn't managed to sleep much in the bed that wasn't designed for someone of his size, but his troubled mind had been the main cause of his restlessness. He had picked at the breakfast and when the deputy came to take the plate away he told Ryan that the marshal had been in the office for some time and he wasn't in a good mood. So Ryan wasn't surprised that the marshal was grim faced when he came to the cells and told Ryan that he had made a decision. There was a long pause before he spoke again.

'You've given me a real problem, Ryan, because I have always prided myself on being consistent with my handling of situations. What you did last night was a clear case of threatening to murder a man.'

'Bryce wanted trouble, Marshal, and I admit that I lost control, but I couldn't promise that I wouldn't do it again in the same situation.'

'It's probably best that you don't make things worse for yourself, boy, at least not whilst I'm trying to help you.'

Ryan took the hint from the marshal and didn't interrupt again even when the marshal was downright insulting and suggested that he was 'pea brained'. When the insults and admonishment had been delivered the marshal decided to let Ryan go, but made it clear that it was more for his ma's benefit than Ryan's. He hoped there wouldn't be a next time.

*

During the ride home Ryan had reminded himself how lucky he had been, but his guilty feelings were heightened when he was greeted by a worried looking Ma. She had expected him home yesterday, but she didn't scold him too much or ask where he'd been.

Ma had loaded his plate with more beans and eggs than usual, but this time he tucked into his second breakfast of the day and the plate was left clean before he headed outside. He needed to keep busy and set about chopping the logs he'd gathered together from some tree felling he'd done with Uncle Tom. By the time he'd stacked the last of the logs in the shed near the cabin he was ready for a ride out to check on the herd.

The herd were grazing close to the stream and he rode amongst them to check that none were lame or looking undernourished. The shallow stream provided all the water that the herd needed and there was no sign of it drying up as had happened just three years ago. Uncle Tom had been on the point of moving on then, but with the help of the bank had managed to struggle through a difficult time.

Satisfied that all was well with the herd he changed his mind about going to the canyon to practise his shooting, figuring that his gun had nearly landed him in enough trouble. He was about to set off for home when he saw the rider approaching from the top of the canyon. He had seen her from a distance several times since he had removed the stone from her horse's hoof and she had

48

waved to him. She was wearing a different outfit and she looked so confident and in control of a horse that was bigger than his own and powerfully built. He wondered what she would think if she knew that he had christened her Miss Snooty. Perhaps if she stopped to talk he might even find out her proper name and who her relatives were.

She pulled up her mount at the same time as he pulled on the reins of his sorrel and she smiled before she said, 'Are you off to frighten the animals again with your pistol shooting in the canyon? I saw you last week and you're good.'

'Not today, I was just checking on my herd. How's your wounded horse?'

'It's fine; I never did thank you properly. Perhaps I can offer you some of my picnic food if you haven't already eaten.'

Ryan lied when he told her that he had left the cabin to inspect the herd without having breakfast and they settled down on the short grass. He helped her unbuckle her saddle-bags containing the packages of food and a small tablecloth and carried them to a shady spot under a nearby tree.

'The name's Ryan Buchanan, by the way and I'd like to know the name of the pretty lady who's kindly sharing her food with me.'

'I already know who you are.' she replied and then told him that her name was Melissa. She didn't reveal who her family were and he didn't pry.

During the weeks following their picnic together they

met on most days and discovered they had a shared interest in horses and that they had both lost their parents although neither probed the circumstances. He teased her and she'd laughed when he told her about the Miss Snooty tag he'd given her. She seemed caring when she asked if he missed his uncle because she had heard about his recent death, but he told her that he was coping well and then changed the subject. She teased him when he revealed how he liked to read and had a special interest in history.

'I thought all cowboys were dumb,' Melissa mocked when he told her some facts about the land claims.

'I didn't mean to bore you,' Ryan replied. She laughed before she told him that he was far from boring and then added, 'But I am puzzled why you have never tried to kiss me after all the time we have spent together. You don't strike me as a shy type.'

'I'm just not used to you city girls and I thought you only wanted to talk about horses,' Ryan replied and smiled before he moved his face close to hers and then paused before he briefly kissed her on the lips. Ryan had no real experience of girls, but he could tell that she wanted him to repeat it so he gently eased her onto her back and kissed her again. She groaned as his hands explored her body beneath her dress, but she gently eased his hand away when it reached under her skirt and then told him that she must be getting back home.

His disappointment was replaced by surprise after she stood up and said, 'You'll have to come to my barn dance party on Saturday.'

'My feet are a bit big for dancing. I tried it last year in

the church hall and the girls went home with bruised toes,' he joked and then asked if it was for something special like a birthday.

'Nothing special, except I like dancing and there's plenty of people of our age who'll be coming, but if you have something else planned—'

'No, I'd like to come, as long as you don't mind clumsy feet.'

'Good! I'm sure my feet will be all right. It'll start about 8 o'clock, but you can come early if you like.'

'I've never taken a girl, I mean a woman, to a dance before, but I expect you've been to lots of dances back East with those smooth city dudes.'

'Too many to remember,' she replied and laughed. 'So, it's a date.'

'I guess so,' he agreed and pulled her close and kissed her again and he heard her sigh, but was disappointed again when she pushed him away and told him that she really did need to be getting home.

She had mounted and started to ride off when he shouted after her and asked where the dance was.

'It's at my grandfather's barn on the Stratton Ranch. See you on Saturday, neighbour.'

Ryan had suspected that Melissa was connected to the Stratton family in some way and he wondered what the major would say about her being friendly with him, especially if he knew that he had beaten up one of his workers. Maybe Melissa wasn't snooty, but the major certainly was and he wouldn't take too kindly to her associating with someone like Ryan who wasn't a rich city dude or a smart young army officer from a well-to-do family. He wondered if his invitation was part of some plot devised by the major to soften him up in the hope of persuading Ryan to talk Ma into selling the land. He didn't trust Major Stratton and perhaps Ryan's friendship with the lovely young woman had been deliberately arranged. And yet he couldn't forget how she had reacted while they were kissing. He would go to the dance on Saturday, if the major's men allowed him in.

Karl Kruger stood in Major Stratton's study and listened carefully as he received his special instructions regarding the barn dance being organized by the major's granddaughter, Melissa.

Kruger had been Stratton's one and only foreman and he'd been well paid for his loyalty.

Kruger was forty-two years old with a stern face that rarely smiled. He was tall and broad shouldered and could get the better of most men when it came to brawling. His wife had left him more than ten years ago because she hated the loneliness of living in the cabin on the Stratton ranch and since then he'd only kept the company of saloon girls. His wife had also deserted her son, Mark, who she'd had with her first husband who had been killed during a raid on the stagecoach that he had ridden shotgun on. Kruger had treated the boy like his own and with the major's help he had been privately educated and been sent off to a military academy when he was eighteen years old just over a year ago.

'I want you to keep a watchful eye on things after I've left the barn, Kruger. I've promised Melissa that I won't stay long. I expect young Mark to be her escort for the evening and fend off any horny ranch-hand that might forget who she is. And I don't want any liquor being consumed. Is all that clear?'

'There won't be any trouble, Major. You need have no worries on that score. Mark will make sure that Melissa is treated like the young lady she is. I think they have spent a lot of time together since he arrived home on leave. They seem to get on well and I think she welcomes the company of someone who is like-minded and educated like herself.'

'My granddaughter is headstrong and has some strange ideas and Mark is a serious young man. I was asking him about his training the other day and he seemed a bit jumpy and nervous and not exactly enthusiastic. Is everything all right?'

Kruger told the major that Mark was fine and was probably tired from the gruelling training that he had been undergoing, but he'd had his own concerns about him since he'd been home.

Stratton liked Kruger's stepson, but he had no breeding and would be totally unsuitable as a suitor for Melissa. He was pleased that Melissa had made it clear that she found Mark boring with his tales of the military.

EIGHT

Major Stratton wished his granddaughter wasn't so rebellious at times, but perhaps it wasn't surprising because her late mother had been just the same, as had her father who had been the major's only child. Melissa's mother had married a no-good against his advice following the death of his son and her new husband had strangled her whilst she slept when he was in a drunken stupor.

Stratton hadn't objected to his young cowhands being invited to the special party organized by Melissa, but he didn't approve of Ryan Buchanan. He'd questioned her about him and she'd told him that he'd helped her when her horse had gone lame when she was out riding. She hadn't told him how much she liked Ryan because he was so different to the young men that had been invited to her Aunt Muriel's social gatherings back East. He hoped that her friendship with Buchanan was just a passing phase and that she would soon grow tired of him, otherwise he would have to arrange to put an end to it.

Major Stratton looked on as Melissa welcomed her young

guests with Mark Kruger standing by her side. Mark was tall and on the thin side and his black hair was cut short. Some of the girls nearly giggled when they saw him in his smart military uniform that made him look out of place compared to the other young men who were all dressed in casual clothes.

The major had been hoping that Ryan wouldn't turn up and was disappointed when he arrived just as he was leaving the barn. He scowled at Ryan and headed back to his magnificent house a short distance away just like he had agreed with Melissa. Karl Kruger had been reminded of his instruction to keep a discreet watch on things and to make sure that nothing should spoil the evening. The cowhands had been told that no liquor was to be brought into the barn and the only drink that was being served was the punch that was in two very large bowls on the long table that also contained ample supplies of food. Some of the ranch-hands had visited the saloon in town and had received a stern warning from Kruger and a few had been barred from entering. One cowhand had accidentally fallen over while dancing with one of Melissa's friends and he'd left with a frightened look on his face after Kruger had whispered in his ear.

Stratton wouldn't have been pleased to see that young Melissa only had eyes for one young man at the dance and that was Ryan. She had left Mark Kruger looking lost and receiving disapproving looks from his pa.

Melissa and Ryan had just finished their third dance together when Paul Bryce approached them. His face still bore some slight scars from the beating that Ryan had given him and Melissa looked in the direction of

Kruger who was watching them, but he didn't move. Ryan braced himself ready for trouble from the man he had threatened to kill and there was a moment of tension before Bryce addressed him.

'I just wanted to say that I was sorry for starting the trouble between us and I don't blame you for what you did to me. I also wanted to warn you that there some around here who might what to cause trouble for you.'

'Thanks, buddy, and I'm sorry for roughing you up like I did,' replied Ryan who then offered his hand to his former foe. Bryce accepted the gesture and looked relieved that he'd made his peace. Ryan watched Bryce rejoin some of his buddies on the other side of the barn, wondering what he meant about others who might want to cause him trouble.

When Ryan told Melissa that he'd needed to make a move before it was too dark to ride home she suggested that he could spend the night in the bunkhouse. The idea would have sounded ridiculous before he and Bryce had shaken hands, but Ryan still wondered if Kruger would be agreeable to him staying. Melissa told him not to worry about Kruger because she would go and tell him that it had all been arranged. Ryan watched, as did most of the other men, as she walked over to Kruger. The ranch foreman didn't appear to say much in response to the news that Ryan would be staying, but he looked none too pleased. All eyes were on Melissa again as she walked back towards Ryan, the tight-fitting clothes showing the shapeliness of her young body. She wasn't unaware of the attention she was receiving.

Kruger had waited until Melissa was back beside Ryan

and then he beckoned his son to come over and didn't hide his disappointment with him when he spoke.

'Why are you standing around like a lemon and letting Buchanan grab Melissa's attention. You are supposed to be her escort. Go and ask her for a dance and show her that you really like her as a woman and not just a friend. By the way you look damned stupid in that uniform. This is a dance not a passing out parade and you should have dressed like everyone else.'

'I've never been good at dancing, Pa, and I was a bit awkward when we danced when we first came in. I could tell she didn't like dancing with me.'

Kruger looked towards the barn's rafters to show his despair and told Mark to just copy what the others were doing and relax. He should try and flatter Melissa and tell her how pretty she was. Mark didn't bother telling Kruger that he was no good at talking to women either, but he didn't and just trudged away.

Mark Kruger was thinking that there was no pleasing his pa at times and he would have been glad to have gone back to his barracks in a few days, but he couldn't. He wondered and worried how his pa would take the news when he told him. He'd been accused of being a coward and perhaps they were right because so far he hadn't even had the courage to tell his pa that he had been sent away from the military academy in disgrace. Perhaps he really would try his best to win over Melissa's affections and then he could use her as an excuse for not returning to the barracks and hope that the real reason never came out. He had already decided that trying to compete with Ryan Buchanan tonight wouldn't be a good idea. He would bide his time and if he had to he would make sure that Ryan wouldn't get in his way to win over Melissa.

Melissa's friends and the other girls had either retired to bed or been driven home by their parents when the last dance was announced by the leader of the band. Ryan and Melissa danced a slow waltz even though the tune was intended for livelier dancing. Major Stratton wouldn't have been pleased if he found out that Kruger had left ten minutes before the dance was over along with his son Mark and that they had looked miserable. In contrast, Melissa had never been happier as she left the barn with Ryan and they headed to the main house which was now in darkness.

Ryan heard the shouting and it took a while to realize where he was. When he did he knew that he was in trouble, because he'd just remembered the warning that Bryce had given him in the barn.

'You are one evil son of a bitch. You've killed a man who was prepared to forget what you did to him,' Kruger shouted into his face.

Ryan tried to struggle to his feet, but he was beaten down by the flurry of punches from the men whose faces were filled with hate. He drifted into unconsciousness, but when he came to he saw the dead, staring eyes of Bryce who was covered in blood and lying beside him. Ryan's distinctive pearl handled pistol was next to him and it was streaked with Paul Bryce's blood.

'Johansen, go and fetch the marshal,' Kruger ordered, 'and tell him to get here quick because some of the boys are itching to hang this excuse for a human being from the rafters in the barn.'

'Then why don't we just do it and bury him somewhere. We could say he left last night,' Rob Slaney suggested.

'It's what he deserves,' Kruger replied and looked as though he was considering letting his men take care of things, but then added, 'Major Stratton is too law abiding and if he found out we'd all be looking for new jobs. So, go and get the marshal like I said.'

NINE

Marshal Clancy was at an important early morning meeting with the mayor and the town council when Johansen burst into his office and told the deputy that Ryan Buchanan had killed Paul Bryce. Deputy Collins was all of a fluster at first, but when he'd calmed down he wrote a note for the marshal and rode out to the Stratton ranch with Johansen. Mick Johansen told him that he and Rob Slaney had witnessed the fight, but they were too late to stop Ryan battering the life out of their buddy.

When Deputy Collins arrived at the Stratton ranch he found the mood amongst some of the Stratton ranch-hands threatening, but Kruger kept them in order. Kruger told them that their buddy's killer would swing from a rope after the law had dealt with him. Ryan had stopped protesting his innocence because he was in a state of confusion and couldn't remember struggling with anyone. Perhaps he really had killed Bryce, but it didn't make sense. His head hurt like hell and he wondered if a blow had scrambled his brain. He'd heard stories of soldiers in the war who had big gaps in their memory after they had suffered head injuries in battle.

Deputy Collins had kept his gun trained on his prisoner while Ryan mounted his sorrel that had been brought from the stables. The deputy had made sure that Ryan's hands were bound, but he would still be able to steer the sorrel on the ride back to town.

When Ryan had seen his horse it had brought back memories of Melissa and their time together last night. He wondered what she would think when she heard the news – if she hadn't already.

During the ride to town the deputy asked Ryan what the fight had been about and when Ryan said that he couldn't remember the deputy had some advice for him.

'If that's your only line of defence, buddy, then I guess you are in big trouble, especially after that beating you gave him in the saloon.'

Major Stratton's disapproving look had been tame compared to Marshal Clancy's when he looked up from his desk and saw Ryan and the deputy.

'Lock him up and then ride out and tell Meg Buchanan what's happened and how this selfish young man has let her down because he can't control his temper.'

Ryan felt a sickness in his belly. In all the commotion and confusion he hadn't thought of Ma and the fresh grief that the news would bring her.

61

'I thought after our talk you would have come to your senses, Buchanan, but I guess you are one selfish, ungrateful son of a bitch as well as a dumb ass.'

Marshal Clancy had ridden out to the Stratton ranch and spoken to the two men who had been in the bunkhouse with Bryce and Buchanan. Mick Johansen and Rob Slaney told him that when they came back from town the dance had finished and they headed straight for the bunkhouse. Buchanan came in and he and Bryce started arguing about Melissa. Bryce was getting the better of Buchanan until the no-good whacked Bryce across the face with his pistol and then clubbed him three of four times as he lay on the floor. Johansen and Slaney told the marshal that they overpowered Buchanan and tied him to his bed. Bryce was beyond help and the men decided to wait until the morning and then told Kruger what had happened. Ryan had managed to free himself and was on the point of escaping when some of the ranch-hands came in from guarding the herd and attacked him when they saw what he had done to Bryce.

Marshal Clancy had hoped that his visit to the Stratton ranch might have meant that he could give Meg Buchanan some reason to hope that Ryan might escape with just a prison sentence, but she would soon have another grave to visit.

Ryan had been struggling once more to try and remember what had happened between him and Bryce when the deputy appeared at his cell door. Ma was with him.

He could tell that she had been crying and her face was pale. Soon fresh tears appeared in her eyes and she peered though the bars of the cell and offered her hand to him. He gently squeezed her fingers and when he spoke his voice choked with emotion for the fresh trouble he had caused her.

'I've let you down, Ma, and I'm sorry. I never wanted to kill Bryce and the worst part is that I don't remember doing it.'

'Oh, Ryan, what do you mean you can't remember? Was it the drink that caused you to take another man's life?'

He told her that he hadn't been drinking, but couldn't offer her an explanation because he just didn't know, although he admitted to having changed since the death of his uncle.

Meg left the cells promising to visit Ryan tomorrow and she couldn't hold back the tears even though she knew it would hurt him so much. She was still crying when the marshal greeted her as she came though into his main office.

'I'm sorry for your latest upset, Meg. Come and sit down before you head back home and tell me if there's anything we can do to help.'

She dabbed away the tears with a small handkerchief containing a floral pattern that she had designed and stitched herself before she replied, 'Thank you, Marshal. Ryan tells me that he's being well looked after. I can manage at the homestead. There are no big jobs to be done because Ryan worked non-stop after I lost my Tom. I think he did it to keep his mind off things. He would have needed some help with the herd, but John Scully has promised he would provide it. So, what's going to happen to Ryan, Marshal?'

The marshal took a deep sigh as he prepared to answer the question he had been dreading. 'He'll have to go to trial, Meg, and then it will be up to the jury. Ryan was provoked when he gave Bryce that beating in the saloon and that might sway the jury in his favour.'

'I think you are trying to be kind to me, Marshal, and I appreciate it, but I think we both know that it will take a miracle if Ryan isn't going to pay the full price for what he's done.'

The marshal couldn't find any more words of comfort and he was relieved when Meg said she needed to get back home. She bid him farewell, but not before she thanked him once again for his support and kindness.

Ryan lay on his cell bed after Ma left, thinking about Melissa and his earlier suspicion that she might have been used to soften him up into getting his ma to sell the land. Was it all planned to get him to the Stratton place so that he could be blamed for killing Bryce? Melissa seemed genuine, but he had no experience of women and had heard older men talk about how women could be wily in ways that men couldn't and they could outfox a man to get what they wanted. Ryan hoped he was wrong about Melissa, but he guessed he would never see her again and so perhaps it didn't matter. He drifted off to sleep, but was woken by voices coming from the main part of the office. He strained his ears to listen, but couldn't hear the details. He heard a woman's voice and he wondered if Ma had returned.

Things quietened down and he was about to settle back on the hard bed when the adjoining door to the cells opened and the marshal approached, leading two people to his cell. One of them was Major Stratton and the other was Melissa. She smiled at him.

'Buchanan, I guess you are entitled to hear what brought these good folks here even though their reasons are quite different. Perhaps the major should have his say first.'

'Buchanan, my usually sensible granddaughter thinks she can help by lying for you and I hope that you will spare her reputation by telling her that she is misguided and just plain silly.'

Melissa angrily told her grandfather that she wasn't a child and she was only telling the truth and this was more important than a blot on her reputation.

The marshal called a halt to the arguing and tried to explain the situation to Ryan.

'According to the men who claim that they saw you kill Bryce it happened soon after the barn dance finished, but Miss Stratton claims that you were with her in her room until sunup.'

Ryan looked at Melissa as he struggled to respond, sensing the glare of the major and the questioning look of the marshal who, after waiting for Ryan's response, asked him if it was true. He felt fresh guilt for suspecting that she had been involved in some plot to get the Buchanan land because now he knew that wasn't so.

Ryan faced Melissa and hesitated before he said, 'I

appreciate you coming here, Melissa, because I can see that it has caused you some grief.' He then turned to the marshal and confessed, 'The truth is, Marshal, I don't remember being in Melissa's room. Just like I don't remember getting into a fight with Bryce because we shook hands at the dance and it doesn't make sense that it would have started up again.'

'Well that settles it,' said the major huffily and then continued, 'If he can't remember anything then it means he's trying to forget what a horrible thing he did to that decent young man. Come on, Melissa, we're going home.'

Melissa gave Ryan a sad and disappointed look. The major looked relieved when he apologized to the marshal for wasting his time.

'You did the right thing, Major, and there's no need to apologize. Your granddaughter has presented very important information. It wouldn't be right if a man ended up at the end of a rope just because he'd lost his memory. I guess it will be up to the jury, but I don't see why they wouldn't believe a fine respectable young lady like Melissa who was prepared to risk her reputation by coming here.'

The major looked troubled as he realized that some of the town's gossips would have a field day when the news spread that Melissa had allowed a man to spend the night in her bedroom. The revelation wouldn't do her future marriage prospects any good either because she would be regarded as no better than a common saloon girl of easy virtue.

'But surely my granddaughter won't have to testify in

court if Buchanan doesn't remember being with her. Can't you see that she has made this up just to protect him? She's just a foolish and naïve girl who thinks she might be in love.'

The marshal wasn't about to be browbeaten by the major and replied, 'She'd be a crucial witness for the defence just like your men would be for the prosecution. If your granddaughter is telling the truth, Major, then it means that your men were lying. Perhaps one of them killed Bryce and arranged some kind of a cover up.'

'Now you're being ridiculous, Marshal,' retorted the major, his face reddening with frustration at not being able to resolve the mess that his granddaughter had created.

'To tell you the truth, Major, I wasn't altogether happy with your men's version of events. I'd appreciate it if you make sure that Johansen and Slaney will be available for me to talk to again. I've got a few things that need attending to, but I'd like to see them this evening or maybe early tomorrow if I get held up.'

'Don't you worry, Marshal, I'll make sure that they are brought to you whenever you call. Perhaps after you've spoken to them you'll accept what I have been telling you and not involve my granddaughter in any of this.'

The major left the area of the cells and Melissa followed him, but not before she had taken a final look at Ryan who still looked baffled by what had gone on. Despite his predicament he smiled at the thought of what Ma would say if it came out that he spent the night with Melissa. The smile soon disappeared at the realization that he was still likely going to hang because the major would put a stop to Melissa's idea of trying to help him. Major Stratton had made it clear that he was more interested in saving Melissa's reputation than Ryan's life.

TEN

Ryan wondered what the two ranch-hands who claimed to have witnessed him killing Bryce would say to the marshal when he told them about Melissa's statement that he couldn't have done it. So he was disappointed to hear that the marshal hadn't made the visit and was still in his office when Ryan's grub was delivered by the deputy. He had mulled over and over the surprise visit of Melissa earlier. He liked Melissa and she'd seemed to be sweet on him, but he suspected she was just playing with him because he was different to the sort of city dudes and college boys that her grandfather would have approved of. She would have had a chaperone until she had started to rebel, but why would she lie for him and invite trouble from her grandfather and become the subject of gossip? None of it made sense, even if he had spent the night with her. He remembered the last dance and walking her to the door of the big house. He remembered when they'd kissed during the last meeting when they were out riding. He'd felt her body tremble and she'd groaned with pleasure when he'd touched her in places that

churchgoing girls would have felt guilty about. He could-
n't remember lying next to her in her bed, although he
had imagined it often enough.

Perhaps he should have lied and told the marshal that
it was just as Melissa had described and maybe the
marshal would have had to let him go. He hoped he
hadn't let Melissa down and that Ma would manage if he
never returned home. Most of all he hoped that he could
escape because he had been thinking about what Bryce
had said about someone who was connected to the
Stratton ranch wishing him harm. Was his uncle's death
just an argument that had got out of hand, fuelled by
liquor, or was it connected with what Bryce had warned
him about?

It was nearly dusk when the marshal returned from the
Stratton ranch. His deputy offered to brew him some
coffee, but the marshal told him to go and check out the
saloon for troublemakers. The marshal had some more
serious thinking to do like he'd done on the ride back,
and he needed to make a decision. He had made mistakes in his early days as a lawman, but with experience
and his commonsense approach he had learned how to
manage most situations. It would be easy to let others
decide Ryan's fate, but avoiding responsibility or desert-
ing his principles wasn't in Clancy's nature.

Marshal Clancy was still sat at his desk with a troubled
look on his face when the deputy returned and asked
him if everything was all right. The marshal gave a heavy
sigh and replied, 'As right as it's going to be. Go and
bring Buchanan out here. I need to have a word with

him before we let him go and before you ask, it's a long story. So, don't tell him anything.'

When the deputy returned with Ryan the marshal nodded towards the chair in front of his desk, inviting him to sit down and then told his deputy not to be a dumb ass and put away the pistol he was pointing at Ryan. The strain was showing on Ryan's face and that wasn't surprising considering what he probably thought was going to happen to him.

'I've got a big problem, young Ryan. I don't know whether that Stratton girl, who is obviously sweet on you, if that's what they call it, was lying to save your skin or is telling the truth. The fact is it may not matter now.'

Ryan gave the marshal a puzzled look and asked him what he meant by the remark.

'Well, I rode out to the Stratton place to talk to those two that said they saw you club Bryce to death and they've disappeared without telling anyone and didn't even wait to collect their pay. Kruger didn't see anything, which means that the only witness that could be called at your trial would be Melissa Stratton. I'm going to release you, but if those two ranch-hands ever turn up then I'll arrest you and leave it to the court. For what it's worth my gut instinct is that we'll never see them around these parts ever again. Your horse is down at Dom's livery, but I don't expect you'll be riding home tonight. You are welcome to bed down in your cell until morning and if you want I would be happy to ride out with you and explain things to Meg.'

Ryan was stunned as the news sunk in that he was a free man. He accepted the marshal's offer to ride home with him in the morning and also opted to bed down in his cell. Although he was relieved at the unexpected outcome, he was still confused about the whole thing, and he had a question for the marshal.

'If I didn't kill Bryce, then who did, Marshal?'

The marshal pondered the question for a while before he replied, 'There's something strange going on between your family and Major Stratton. I get the impression that the major doesn't like you very much and I'm not sure if it's just because he doesn't approve of you paying his lovely granddaughter attention. I think if he had his way he'd pack her off back East, but that young woman has a mind of her own.'

'My Uncle Tom told me all about the major's obsession with trying to buy our land so that he could boast that all the land from the base of the Deal Mountains down to the Mersey River belonged to him. I thought perhaps he'd given up on the idea and he was kind to us after Uncle Tom was killed.'

The marshal gave a cynical smile and told Ryan that in his experience men like Major Stratton usually had a motive when they showed acts of kindness.

ELEVEN

Ryan was grateful that the marshal had offered to ride home with him and explain to his ma what had happened. Things had been strained between Ryan and his ma when she'd visited him in his cell. She still couldn't understand why he couldn't remember what had happened, but stopped short of accusing him of lying. She had also made it clear that she thought he should mix with people of his own kind and not girls like Melissa Stratton who was too snooty for Ma's liking. Ryan knew that Ma was suffering from the stress of recent events and he hadn't argued with her because he was still feeling guilty for bringing her fresh grief.

'So what are your plans, now that you have had another very lucky escape?' the marshal asked as they left Main Street and set the horses into a steady trot.

'It's up to Ma really, Marshal. If she wants to stay on at the homestead then I'll be staying for as long as she needs me, but I'm hoping to persuade her to sell up and buy a little cabin close to the town. It would be easier for her to attend church on Sunday and visit the cemetery.

She could have an easier life and meet more people than she does out at the homestead. If she agrees then once she has settled in I aim to do some travelling.'

'It sounds as though you have been doing a lot of thinking in that little cell. Your idea sounds a good one to me and I'm sure your Meg wouldn't want to stand in your way.'

Ryan had been intending to ask the marshal about his pa's death and now seemed a good time. It was something that his uncle had promised to tell him, but never got the chance. The marshal looked serious for a moment after the question had been put to him and took his time in answering.

'I had just returned to my office after doing my rounds on the night your pa was killed in the saloon. Old Jake Haskin hobbled into my office and told me there'd been a shooting in the saloon and when I got there your pa was already dead and must have died quickly. The feller who shot him was a stranger in town and he'd accused your pa of owing him money for a horse he'd sold him way back. Your pa told him that he must have mistaken him for someone else, but the feller wouldn't let it go and things got heated. The feller got really abusive and your pa just snapped I guess and went for his gun, maybe just to shut him up and not intending to shoot, but the feller was really handy with his gun and he shot your pa.'

'So what happened to the feller?' asked Ryan, who was eager to find out as much as possible.

'I couldn't hold him because the witnesses told me that your pa had gone for his gun first. He just rode out of town as if nothing had happened. I guess Jack was in the wrong place at the wrong time or he just had the misfortune to have a double. Jack was a fine man even if he was a bit wild before he mellowed somewhat.'

Ryan was disappointed because he had expected there to have been more to his pa's death. It was just a feeling he had when he had mentioned it to his uncle.

Smoke was coming from the chimney as they approached the cabin and despite the early hour Ma would have already finished her early morning chores. The marshal said that he'd sampled some of Meg's cooking before and he wouldn't be turning down her offer of breakfast that he fully expected her to make.

The marshal spotted the figure in the rocking chair on the porch way and watched her come to greet them, but it wasn't Meg. Ryan had already recognized Mrs Swinburne who was Ma's best friend and was wondering what she was doing there so early in the morning. As Ryan dismounted he started to get an uneasy feeling because there was something different about the place, but he couldn't put his finger on it.

When Mrs Swinburne reached out to hug him he could see that she had been crying and fresh tears appeared.

'I'm so sorry, Ryan. I was expecting my Arthur to come back with the marshal later. Did you pass him on the way?'

'What's happened, Mrs Swinburne? Where's, Ma?' Ryan asked, ignoring the question.

Mary Swinburne couldn't bring herself to answer,

Then the marshal asked her the same question and this time she blurted out a reply.

'I'm sorry, Ryan, but your sweet Ma is dead.'

Ryan jumped on to the porch way and crashed through the front door of the cabin, but he was soon back out and demanding to know where Ma was.

The marshal's face was grave because he had just heard even more dreadful news from the distraught Mary Swinburne, who had now hurried back inside the cabin.

'You may not want to see your ma just now. Let's go inside,' the marshal suggested.

'Marshal, I want to see my ma right now. I'm not some little boy.'

'You're right, son, but there appears to have been some kind of accident in the barn.'

Ryan didn't wait for the marshal to say any more as he ran towards the back of the house and the barn, or at least what remained of it because when it came into view it was just a burnt out shell.

The marshal hurried after Ryan, but he heard the anguished cry before he reached him. Ryan's dog was lying beside Ma and only small patches of its coat remained on its charred body. The smell of burnt flesh was mostly the result of the badly burned bodies of the two horses that Ma had probably tried to rescue.

Ryan gently rubbed away a black smudge on Ma's face, but didn't remove the blanket that had been placed over her charred body by Arthur Swinburne before he'd gone to get the marshal. The marshal put a sympathetic hand on the sobbing Ryan's shoulder and then he walked away to give Ryan a private moment. But the marshal was wondering if it really had been just an accident. When he returned to the barn later he saw something that made him think that the fire may have been started deliberately. He would have to decide whether Ryan should be told about his suspicions or let him believe it was an accident, because it might be impossible to prove otherwise.

TWELVE

Melissa Stratton was usually seen dressed in bright colours, but she still looked stunning as she surveyed herself in the mirror and smoothed the black dress with her hands. Margaret, the housemaid had done a few minor, but skilful adjustments to the dress that her grandfather had ordered for her to wear on special formal occasions. Her grandfather had shown his disapproval when she'd told him that she planned to attend the funeral of Meg Buchanan to offer her support to Ryan because now he had no family.

The major sat stony faced as he and Melissa were driven to the white wooded church in the fine coach that would have been worthy as a royal carriage. The matching black teamsters adorned black ribbons as a sign of respect. The driver looked uncomfortable in his black uniform and the white shirt whose collar was too small for his bulging neck. He was more suited to the role of bodyguard than driver and many suspected that was his main function.

*

78

The marshal sat beside Ryan in the front row of the church, which was well attended, including some like John Appleby who had known Meg since she'd arrived in the town not long after himself. The preacher, Sydney Bowler, had taken over from the old minister, Abe Newton, who had retired soon after Tom Buchanan had been buried. He had discussed Meg's life with Ryan and some older members of his congregation and his tribute was worthy of the kind and respected person that she had been. Ryan had managed to control his feelings until the preacher mentioned the tragic accident that had taken a lovely servant of God from her adopted son, Ryan and many friends. Ryan still didn't believe that Ma's death was an accident after the marshal had said that he ought to know that he'd spotted cheroot stubs near the barn. Tom Buchanan had been a smoker, but the stubs were very recent and couldn't have been his throwaways. Ryan cast his eyes in the direction of the seats close by and the immaculately dressed Major Stratton. The major seemed unaware of the attention that Ryan was showing him as he pondered over the possibility that the major was responsible for his ma's death.

The preacher made just a short tribute at the graveside as he had looked nervously at the gathering clouds and the mourners had made their way to the small hall beside the church. Mary Swinburne and some of her friends would serve tea and a selection of sandwiches to those who had gathered. There would be much talk about Meg and the good deeds that she had done for some of them in their hour of need.

Ryan had stayed beside the grave to have a private moment and he was surprised, but pleased, that Melissa was waiting at the entrance to the cemetery. They walked to the hall together and Ryan was approached by Major Stratton who had been waiting for his granddaughter. He gave Melissa a disapproving look before addressing Ryan.

'Please accept my deepest sympathy, young man. She was a fine lady. I expect that you will be moving on. Perhaps there are too many sad memories for one so young and you will want to explore some of our great country. My offer to buy, what I assume is now all your land, is still open and it is a generous offer.'

The marshal had overheard the major's comments and glowered at him for being so insensitive. He hoped Ryan wouldn't let it get to him and regret causing trouble at such a sad time.

'Major, I thank you for your sympathy, but the land is not for sale. My ma refused to sell you the land and made it clear that she never wanted to do any dealings with you. I don't know why she felt that way, but out of respect to her wishes if ever I should decide to sell the land it will never be to you. I'm sorry and I don't wish to offend you, but that's the way it is.'

The major controlled his annoyance and replied politely that he fully understood Ryan's position and wished him well for the future and then told Melissa that he would wait for her in the carriage.

'What will you do, Ryan?' Melissa asked.

'I honestly don't know, Melissa, but I meant what I said about not selling the land to the major.'

'Don't worry about Grandfather. He's always had this idea of owning your land even though he has no use for it. He'll be disappointed, but he'll get over it.'

Ryan thanked her for coming, and got an unexpected reply when he asked when he would see her again.

'I'm leaving tomorrow to stay with a friend back East and I'll be gone for quite a long time unless we get bored with each other.'

'I expect it's your grandfather's idea to keep us apart,' replied Ryan, unable to hide the disappointment in his voice.

'You should know me better than that, Ryan. This trip has nothing to do with my grandfather and was arranged months ago. Perhaps I'll see you when I get back and I hope everything works out all right for you. Goodbye, Ryan.'

Ryan watched Melissa walk away confused by her varying moods towards him. She seemed to welcome his advances on occasions and then she would keep him at a distance. He wanted to be more than a friend to Melissa, but now he wondered if he would ever see her again.

THIRTEEN

Ryan shook his head after he'd taken a swig from the whiskey bottle as he sat on the porchway of the cabin. He had thought about bringing home the friendly stray dog that he'd seen in town yesterday, but it wouldn't be fair on the dog if he moved on. He remembered trying to teach his first dog tricks when it was just a pup that his Uncle Tom had brought home. Uncle Tom had been drunk when he'd bought it from a traveller who claimed it was bred from two show dogs. He couldn't remember what breed it was, but Meg had scolded him and told him that it looked just like the strays that roamed around town looking for scraps of food.

The empty whiskey bottle fell from his grasp as Ryan became drowsy with the effects of the drink. He felt cold, but decided against going into the cabin.

Ryan just grunted when he felt the first jab in the chest as he lay back in the rocking chair. The second prod was harder and Ryan sat up, and reached for his pistol, but cried out when he felt the hard wrap on his knuckles.

'You'd be dead now, mister, if I intended you real harm.'

Ryan squinted at the figure in front of him as he tried to remove the fuzziness from his brain, 'Mr Kenley, why did you whack me like that?'

'To teach you a lesson, that's why. This is a hostile land we live in and you always need to be on your guard. I only heard about what happened to Meg when I got back yesterday. I've been doing some trapping up at the Deal Mountains. I'm very sorry, son, because she was a special kind of lady.'

Judd Kenley was seventy-two years old and a veteran of the war he had been much too old to fight in, but he had and been left with only one good leg. He was lean and wiry and fit as a fiddle despite his liking for whiskey and a clay pipe that spent more time in his mouth than in his pocket. The beard looked shaggier than the last time Ryan had seen him and the thin hair was almost white and reached his shoulders.

Ryan asked him if his trip had been successful and Judd shook his head. 'These are lean times for hunting. I swear that some of those animals I go after are getting craftier than they used to be, or are somehow passing on a warning when one of them spots one of my traps. I had a bit of luck with the skunks though.'

'You hunt for skunks?' asked Ryan who had never heard of such a thing.

'You bet! I introduced them in the woodland near the mountains a few years ago and although they are not native to these parts they've bred well. I've got a few tied to my mule there.'

'Do they smell like people say?' Ryan asked, his face showing his recollection of what he'd been told about the smell.

Judd laughed before he replied, 'I've known a few people smell worse than a skunk even after they've had a bath. There was a feller I met in the war who used to wash himself in the stream every day, but he was as smelly as they come. They used to call him Skunky, but he just used to laugh.'

Ryan was thinking that old Judd was probably a stranger to soap and water judging by the smell coming from him, but perhaps it was the fur coat he was wearing despite it being a hot day.

'There's a lot of ignorance about the dear old skunk and the little feller doesn't smell like people think. If it's in danger of being attacked it shows its ass to the predator and squirts an oily solution at it and that's what smells foul. It can squirt the stuff ten feet or more.'

'What will you do with those you've trapped?'

'I'll skin them and sell them to John Appleby and he'll sell them on to to some ladies who like to have fur draped over them. I'll eat the meat myself.'

Ryan screwed his face, remembering the earlier comments about the smelly oil.

'It beats the taste of those cattle that you send to market,' said Judd seeing the pained expression on Ryan's face and then added, 'I wouldn't be surprised if one day they don't sell it as what they call a delicacy in those posh restaurants back East. Anyway, young feller, how are you coping? I hope you are not moping about here feeling sorry for yourself.'

'I'm doing OK, Mr Kenley. I just need a bit of time to get used to things.'

'Sure you do, but don't take too long. I was thinking about you a while back when I heard about a tragedy over at Lake Bala. Two young boys were in a canoe when it capsized and they both drowned. It seems that there were lots of onlookers, but none of them could swim. I remember you saving that young boy who fell into the Mersey River and was being swept towards the rapids until you saved him. How old were you, about thirteen I reckon? It must have taken some guts because I also remember your Uncle Tom telling me that you weren't a strong swimmer at the time.'

Ryan was a mite embarrassed and said that he only did what most people would have done from around these parts.

'You're too modest, young Ryan, and your pa was just the same. I don't suppose he ever told you about the time he rescued a comrade who couldn't move after he'd been shot in the leg. Your pa dragged the feller to safety despite getting a bullet in his shoulder.'

'I think I was too young for Pa to be talking about the war, but Ma said that he and Uncle Tom never had much to say about it except that they lost some good friends and brave men died.'

'There were brave men on both sides in those tragic times,' Judd replied with a heavy sigh and then continued, 'Anyway, I had better be getting along, but I'll tell you some more tales when I come by this way again. I don't usually give advice, but I'd lay off that hard liquor if I were you, at least until you get to my age.'

Judd laughed as he hobbled down the steps and when Ryan called after him and asked him to have a bite to eat he had an answer that made Ryan smile.

'Thanks for the offer, boy, but I can smell those skunks from here and I think they've started cooking already.'

Ryan watched Judd trek towards the mule with the aid of a stout stick. He wondered what tales others would have of the man who always looked on the brighter side of life. Ryan felt better than he had done since Ma's funeral, but he would soon be turning to the bottle again to bring him some comfort.

FOURTEEN

Ryan had been in the saloon for three nights running and when he entered the crowded bar he hoped that he would have a change of luck and the man would be there. Vicky greeted him with her usual smile and waited until he'd ordered his first beer before she sidled over and kissed him on the cheek.

'You don't look happy, handsome. Is that snooty Stratton girl giving you a hard time?'

'Melissa's just a friend, Vicky and no more than that.' Ryan replied, his tone was subdued because he had more important things on his mind than girls at the moment.

Vicky gave him a disbelieving look and replied, 'Yeah, sure she is. I saw you holding hands outside the general store once and when you were saying goodbye it didn't look like just a friendly kiss you gave her.'

Ryan smiled at Vicky as he recalled the chance meeting he'd had with Melissa, but his face became serious when he saw a man coming down the stairs with one of Vicky's girls.

'See you later, handsome,' said Vicky and made her

way across the saloon.

Jonty, the saloon owner, who sometimes worked as a barman, had been watching Ryan and leaned forward before he spoke, 'We don't want any trouble, Ryan, and I hope you are not thinking of starting anything because you're rather outnumbered.'

Ryan took a gulp of beer before he replied and when he did he lied. 'I'm not looking for trouble, Jonty.'

'Good,' said a relieved Jonty, because he liked Ryan and he didn't want to see him come to grief at the hands of the Stratton boys, or have to ban him from the saloon.

Ryan watched the man and girl as they reached the bottom of the stairs. The girl smiled at the men seated at the table and then walked away as he rejoined his buddies and sat down. The man hadn't looked in Ryan's direction until the man next to him nudged him and nodded towards Ryan.

'What are you staring at, kid?' Rawlins growled.

'I was trying to decide where the smell was coming from because there wasn't any until you came downstairs.' Ryan replied.

Rawlins' buddies sniggered, but he wasn't amused as he struggled to find a suitable reply.

'You've got a big mouth, kid.'

Ryan smiled and said, 'I was just wondering if you paid the girl extra for putting up with that smell.'

'Perhaps you're trying to make up for not helping your uncle that night when I plugged him,' Rawlins accused and then looked at his buddies and added. 'Yeah, that's what he's trying to do.'

'I'm not looking for trouble, Rawlins, just doing a bit

of teasing like you did that night. Like I said, I don't want any trouble.'

'Well I think you've found some, kid.'

'Leave it, Rawlins,' advised one of his buddies and then reminded him about the warning that Kruger had passed on from the major.

Rawlins' face showed his anger and he snapped, 'I'm not letting this go because I don't want the kid shooting me in the back to ease his guilt.'

'Back off, Rawlins,' Jonty ordered, sensing trouble and then added, 'You heard what Ryan said. He doesn't want any trouble.'

Rawlins ignored the saloon owner, stood up and moved towards Ryan, his face flushed by his feeling that he was being humiliated by a young kid.

'I wasn't wrong about the smell. It's really strong. Just to show that I don't want any trouble, here's a dollar so you can go and have a bath over at Tim's Barber Shop.'

Ryan didn't take his eyes off Rawlins as he placed the dollar coin on the bar with his left hand. It was the last straw for Rawlins who whipped out his pistol. Rawlins' hand had gripped the handle of the weapon before Ryan had moved his own hand at lightning speed to draw his pistol and fire a shot into Rawlins' face. Rawlins was dead before he fell close to the bar.

'Jesus,' Jonty cried out from his position behind the bar then called for someone to go and fetch the marshal and the doc.

Ryan looked in the direction of the table of Rawlins' buddies, but they made no attempt to move. One of them raised a hand as though to signal that they didn't intend to get involved.

Ryan holstered his gun, but kept watch on the two Stratton boys in case they changed their mind, but they didn't.

The marshal, his deputy and the doc arrived at the same time. The marshal looked angry when he addressed Ryan, 'I don't need to ask if it was you who shot Rawlins, do I? And I don't need to ask the doc if he's dead. Deputy, go and get Moses and tell him there's some business for him. I expect Major Stratton will be paying for the funeral.'

The marshal pulled Ryan's gun from its holster and then announced that he was going to lock Ryan up in the cells and then he would come back and question everyone who was there. No one was to leave the saloon until he got back.

'Hold on, Marshal,' Jonty pleaded on Ryan's behalf 'You might save yourself a lot of time if you listen to what happened here.'

'Let's have it then,' replied the marshal without showing much interest.

'Ryan did a bit of teasing about Rawlins being smelly, which he was, God rest his soul. Rawlins didn't see the funny side and started spoiling for trouble even though the kid told him he didn't want any. Rawlins' buddies even told him to back off, but he wouldn't and went for his gun first. Ryan was just too fast for him, otherwise he'd be lying on the floor instead of Rawlins.'

The marshal faced the two men just after he'd seen the doc shake his head and confirm that Rawlins was dead. The marshal hadn't needed a doctor to tell him that a man with half his face missing was dead.

'So is it true?' the marshal asked the Stratton men and when they only nodded their head in agreement the marshal repeated his question, but in a much louder voice that demanded an answer.

'Yeah, it was just like Jonty said,' answered the skinny one of the two. The marshal faced the other man and he got the same answer, but in a stuttering voice, because he was still shocked by the sight of Rawlins' blood.

'So who drew first?' the marshal asked to make sure that there was no doubt.

'Rawlins went for his gun first but the kid was so fast. I don't think I've seen anyone draw as a quick,' the skinny one answered.

'That's all I need. If the word gets out that we've got a kid gunfighter in town it'll attract all kinds wanting to take him on,' the marshal sighed as he handed Ryan his gun and then delivered a warning.

'I want you to ride home, Ryan and the next time you come into town stay out of trouble or I'll ban you from ever returning. Is that clear?'

'No worries, marshal. I'll do just like you say,' replied a relieved Ryan, even though he had been prepared to face any punishment that might have been given to him.

Ryan left the saloon with the marshal shaking his head as he watched him step outside, wondering if Ryan Buchanan might become a whole heap of trouble.

Ryan's hopes that killing Rawlins would give him a fresh start didn't last long and his drinking habit became worse. He'd tossed away the empty whiskey bottle just before he'd ridden down Main Street. It was just a week after Rawlins had been buried and as Ryan pushed open the saloon door he gave no thought to the warning the marshal had given him.

Vicky gave him her usual smile, but she didn't approach him because her experience told her that he was in a black mood and not interested in her or any other woman's company. Jonty looked troubled when he served Ryan his first drink and didn't get a response after he had given Ryan his usual friendly greeting. Ryan was preoccupied with weighing up the groups of men who were sat at the tables either playing cards or just chin-wagging. He glowered at the man who was fondling one of the saloon girls and was thinking that perhaps he ought to teach him a lesson about respecting a woman.

A young feller had been admiring Ryan's pistol and he asked him what make it was because he was really interested in it.

'Mind your own goddamn business,' Ryan snapped and the young feller turned and walked away, not risking a confrontation.

'Go easy, Ryan. I think you should make that your last drink and go and sleep it off,' advised Jonty in a low voice, but wasn't surprised when Ryan replied, 'I'll go when I'm ready. I didn't ask that feller to disturb me.'

'Just go easy, that's all I'm saying,' Jonty repeated and then walked to the other end of the bar to attend to some customers, leaving Ryan just staring ahead with a morose expression on his face.

The saloon owner was relieved when Ryan took a final swig from his glass and headed for the door, but his relief was short lived when Ryan stumbled against the chair of one of the men playing cards. The man picked up the card that had fallen to the floor, shook his head and said, 'Another boy who should still be drinking sarsaparilla.' The rest of the table laughed and one of them said. 'I think he wants to apologize to you, Vinny.'

Apologizing wasn't what Ryan had in mind when he said, 'If you didn't have such a fat ass to go with your ugly face, mister, folks wouldn't bump into you.'

Vinny wasn't smiling like his buddies were when he pushed back his chair and stood up to face Ryan. Vinny's face was pocked-marked and his cross-eyes and oversized nose gave him a look that could best be described like Ryan had said. Vinny stood a good four inches taller than Ryan and was some forty or more pounds heavier.

'You've got a big mouth for a little runt,' Vinny growled and took a swing at Ryan. His large fist smashed into Ryan's face and sent him reeling with blood splashing on to his shirt. Ryan might have avoided the punch had he not been drinking so heavily. He had felt the pain from his broken nose and shook his head to clear it before he rushed towards Vinny and was only caught a glancing blow this time. Ryan delivered a heavy blow to Vinny's belly and followed it with a short uppercut that sent the giant frame of Vinny crashing into the table.

One of Vinny' s buddies staggered to his feet after being sent sprawling, but Vinny ordered his buddies to stay out of it and then added, 'This kid's all mine.'

Vinny flexed his shoulders and clenched both fists and then delivered several vicious blows to Ryan's face. While Ryan was dazed, Vinny put a hand at the back of

Ryan's head, pulled him forward and head butted him three times before letting him fall to the saloon floor.

Vinny hovered over Ryan waiting for him to get up, but when the unconscious Ryan didn't move Vinny spat on him and then told his buddies they were leaving.

Jonty waited until the group had left the saloon and then asked a couple of his regulars to help the bloodied Ryan to a chair.

'Shall I go and get the doc?' one of the men asked, but Ryan was already coming to and Jonty told them to take Ryan into his private room at the back of the saloon and lay him on the couch. The two men were slowly frog marching Ryan towards the owner's private quarters when Jonty stopped them and said he had a better idea.

When Ryan opened his eyes he caught a glimpse of the rich looking velvet curtains before he closed his eyes again. His mouth was dry and his nose was throbbing and some of the weird dreams he'd had came into his thoughts and none of them were pleasant. He didn't remember booking into a hotel room which is where he figured he was now and he didn't remember taking all his clothes off either.

'You've stopped snoring, so I guess you are awake,' said the voice that was close to his ear and belonged to the person lying beside him.

He was too dazed to be startled by the voice and before he turned to face whoever it was he could smell the perfume.

'Who are you?' he asked as he peered though eyelids that wouldn't easily open because of the swelling.

'You aren't much good at sweet-talking a girl, are you Ryan?'

'Janet, is that you?'

'Of course it's me. Who else would be dumb enough to volunteer to nurse you through the night?'

Ryan gave a mumbled thanks and he felt embarrassed as he remembered the fight and the trouble he'd caused.

'I was a fool picking a fight with that big feller, wasn't I?'

Janet smiled before she replied, 'Damn stupid, getting your good looks all messed up. Vinny couldn't have ended up any uglier than he already was.'

Ryan glanced down at Janet who was wearing just the short blouse she'd worn in the bar and he asked, 'Did we do anything in here last night?'

'There you go again hurting my feelings by telling me you don't even remember what happened between us.' Janet replied, faking her anger.

'I'm sorry, but my head isn't working properly yet. Perhaps it will come back to me later. I'm sure it must have been something special because you are a lovely looking girl, Janet. I think I remember telling you that when we were talking on the night of my birthday.'

Ryan's thoughts turned to the night he was supposed to have slept with Melissa and he still couldn't remember that either.

Janet Paulson was nineteen years old and just about the prettiest girl ever to have worked at the saloon. The auburn hair was naturally curly and her pale green eyes had captivated many a man just like her curvy body that had caused some married men to be tempted and many others to part with their money.

'Perhaps when you remember you might want me to be your regular girlfriend and start walking out together. We could even attend church together this coming Sunday and I could wear my best buttoned up dress. I haven't been much of a churchgoer since my. . . .' Janet paused and laughed before she stopped her teasing by saying, 'I'm only kidding you, Ryan. If I turned up for church there wouldn't be many eyes looking at the minster. The womenfolk would be giving me their most evil looks and their men would be staring at these lovely titties of mine.' Janet laughed again as she placed her hands underneath her bosoms and lifted them. For a moment Ryan forgot his pain.

'Did we really do anything last night because if we didn't then I think I'm going to be regretting it?'

'If we did then it was because I like you, Ryan, and not because it was business, but don't go telling anyone because I don't give charity. Anyway, I think you might need your money to pay for the damage downstairs and you'll want to thank Jonty for taking care of you after you took on more than you bargained for with big Vinny. And no, we didn't do anything, but I'm sure we will if you get your looks back.'

Ryan told Jonty that he'd pay for the damage later and declined his offer of an early morning drink. He'd seen his reflection in the mirror that hung on the wall behind the bar and winced when he'd seen his swollen face and his bulbous nose that made him almost unrecognizable from how he looked this time yesterday. He thanked

Jonty for not getting the marshal involved because he figured the marshal had just about run out of patience with him.

FIFTEEN

Deak Mullen hadn't expected to see the man again. He should have told him to keep his money because he was no longer for hire, but he hadn't. He didn't know why he'd intended to stop killing people; he could still outdraw most men when his coughing wasn't troubling him. He'd never believed in all that religious stuff about a day of reckoning. As far as Deak was concerned he'd been born evil and ending his days being a good guy was never going to balance the books. The fact was he was just plain tired, but perhaps not too tired for a final bit of fun.

He hadn't liked the feller who'd handed over the money, but he never did like chicken-livered men who paid others to do their dirty work, although he suspected that this feller was just hiring him for someone else. Mullen had killed some men who deserved to die, including the last one who raped a thirteen-year-old, sweet innocent girl. Her kinfolk wanted him dead, but Mullen did it for the money, not justice.

He took a last look around the rundown cabin that

had been his home for the past seven years because he didn't plan on coming back. Mullen was thirty-eight years old, slim built. His face was thin and lined with a yellowish complexion which he guessed was linked to the cough he'd developed this last year. He'd already saddled the black mare earlier and it snorted as he approached it, perhaps eager to get going because it hadn't been ridden since he'd gone into the nearby town for supplies a month ago.

The light brown dog that had a white tip on its tail walked alongside him as he approached the horse. The dog was ready to run alongside him for a while before it would turn and head back home.

Mullen mounted the horse and grunted with the exertion. The dog yapped as it waited for its master to move off, but it wouldn't be running alongside him today: Mullen drew his pistol and leaned to the side of the horse's neck as he fired a bullet into the dog's head. He holstered the pistol, and then lit a cheroot he'd taken from his pocket, took a long drag on it and then spurred his horse forward. He intended to take the mountain pass that would take him to the trail that led to Carrsville where he would find his next unsuspecting victim.

When Mullen made camp for the night he did like he did most nights and drank a full bottle of hard liquor. A troubled conscience wasn't the reason he couldn't sleep without the help of liquor, he just didn't seem able to sleep like normal folks. He was racking his brain and trying to think about the last time he'd been in Carrsville. It couldn't have been anything special, but few towns were, unless there was a good looking girl in the saloon. He'd always had a woman in his life until the last one just two months ago. He'd treated her well and even put a ring on her finger, but nothing seemed to make her happy, except browsing through the catalogues and ordering more clothes than she'd needed. He couldn't even blame the drink for the night he strangled her and buried her next to the latrine at the back of the cabin they'd shared. The owner of the general store had asked about her and Mullen had told him that she'd run off with a travelling salesman. The storekeeper had looked disappointed because it meant he'd lost his best customer.

Mullen threw the whiskey bottle aside and closed his eyes, but then sat up as he heard the scurrying sound that was coming from near where the bottle had landed.

'Damn,' he muttered to himself as he realized that it was a large rat that was showing interest in the empty whiskey bottle. The reason for his cursing was that he'd forgotten to release the rats that he'd kept as pets. He had been fonder of the rats than the dog he'd shot rather than leave it to fend for itself.

Mullen's arrival in Carrsville brought back a few vague memories, but he didn't see anything special about the town and the feller at the livery who had taken charge of his horse was a miserable son of a bitch. The diner looked tempting, but he had a greater craving for hard liquor than food and so he headed for the saloon. He got the customary wary looking glances from the few men at the bar and he'd never figured out why he frightened most men before they'd seen him in action. Maybe it was the low slung holster of his Colt .45 that made men suspect that his pistol wasn't for shooting rabbits. In some cases it might have been the coldness of his eyes that never looked away when they met the gaze of a stranger.

Mullen had told Jim Peters, who was Jonty's head barman that he was planning on giving his nephew a surprise, but he didn't know what he looked liked. He would be much obliged if the barman gave him a nod if Ryan Buchanan came into the saloon.

The saloon girl, who called herself Margo, had come on really strong and he'd bought her a drink and told her that he would like to do some business later. She'd openly rubbed herself against him and whispered in his ear that he wouldn't forget her after what she had planned for him because there was something about him that she liked.

A group nearby were discussing guns and one of them was bragging about the gun that he had just bought and was demonstrating how smooth the action was. The feller with the new gun had a big mouth and that was something Mullen couldn't abide. He might just shut him up later and make him pee in his pants because he looked the sort who would do that if he faced the prospect of a shoot-out.

He didn't know whether it was the whiskey, or the effects of the journey, but Mullen suddenly felt tired and was thinking of seeking out Margo when he saw the barman give him a nod. The young feller was big, but his face was only slightly marked. His nose must have been

busted once, but he probably hadn't done much brawling. The pearl handled pistol he was wearing was an old
model that had once been Mullen's favourite. In
Mullen's experience most men were easy to goad if they
had been drinking or something personal could be
aimed at them, but this kid looked cold sober and he
held Mullen's stare when he looked at him. He was
tempted to just ask the kid what he was looking at, but
the kid would likely just apologize and that wouldn't do.

Margo, the saloon girl approached the kid and made
a real fuss of him and made it obvious that she wanted
the kid to take her upstairs. Mullen was about to use her
as an excuse for confronting the kid when she turned
and walked away after being turned down by the man
he'd come to kill. Margot had looked real disappointed
as she walked away.

The feller who hired Mullen had warned him that the
kid was handy with a gun and had taken out a feller by
the name of Rawlins. Mullen had seen Rawlins in action
a couple of years ago in a saloon in Teal Creek and he'd
just had an idea of how he would do what he'd been paid
for. He would do the business and claim self defence if
the marshal made an appearance. He hoped to be
upstairs on top of the lovely Margo while the kid was
being getting carried out to the undertaker's.

'Hey, barman, does that sly feller who shot my buddy
Rawlins ever come in here? They tell me he was a young
kid who is always bragging how good he is, but I heard
that he's a sly back-shooter.'

The barman realized that Mullen had tricked him into
identifying Ryan and turned to him to say that he didn't

want any trouble and he should drink up and leave before he sent someone to fetch the marshal.

'I'm not looking for trouble. I just asked a simple question and if the feller I'd like to speak to isn't here then you won't have a problem.'

Ryan turned to face Mullen and said, 'I'm the one you're looking for, mister, but it was your buddy who wanted trouble, just like you do.'

'Well at least you are facing me. I heard you shot Rawlins in the back as he was walking away to avoid the trouble that you started.'

'It wasn't like that,' said the barman, who had been drinking in the saloon on his night off when Ryan shot Rawlins and had seen what happened.

Mullen's face grew angry and his eyes narrowed as he turned to glower at Jim Peters. 'Keep your big, fat, ugly nose out of this, or you've served your last drink.'

Mullen faced Ryan again and gave him a sly smile before he spoke.

'I'm going to play a little game, kid, but I'll give you a chance. I'm going to draw this pistol of mine just to show you what you are up against and then I'll holster it and give you the chance to draw first.' Mullen sniggered and turned towards the table nearby, addressing the group, 'Now that seems fair, doesn't it, boys?' No one in the group answered, they knew that there would soon be blood on the floor.

Mullen moved away from the bar, but before he lowered his hand close to his gun handle Ryan had a warning for him: 'I'm not interested in playing any game, mister, and if you put your hand near your pistol, I'll shoot you.'

'Well that sounds like a threat to me, kid,' replied Mullen and then reached for his gun, but coughed just as he was on the point of firing it as the bullet from Ryan's gun ripped into his throat. Deak Mullen fell on to the saloon floor and his blood spurted from his main artery and then he coughed for the last time. The eyes that he'd thought frightened men now had a look of surprised horror that had appeared at the moment he'd realized that he'd met his match.

'One of you boys go and get the marshal!' shouted the barman as he addressed the group sat at the table. The feller with the new gun got up and said, 'I ain't ever seen anything like that,' and then hurried from the saloon to get the marshal.

'You're best to stay until the marshal gets here, Ryan, but don't worry, that feller was asking for trouble and deserved what he got. He told me he was your uncle.'

Ryan placed his gun on the bar after he'd made sure that Mullen wasn't going to be any more trouble to him and then he accepted a glass of beer from the barman who told him it was on the house.

When the marshal arrived he looked none too pleased even though the man who had gone to fetch him had told him what had happened. He sighed heavily before he addressed Ryan and said, 'Are you sure that trouble isn't your middle name?'

'It wasn't Ryan's fault, Marshal,' pleaded the barman in Ryan's defence.

'Yeah, yeah, so I've heard,' replied the marshal and then knelt down beside the body, taking care to avoid the pool of blood.

When the marshal stood up he gave Ryan one of his famed cynical looks when he asked, 'This killing may not be as simple as it seems. I take it you knew this feller, Ryan?'

'I'd never seen him before he started goading me about Rawlins. Why do you think I should know him, Marshal?' Ryan asked and he was in for a shock when the answer came.

'That's Deak Mullen,' replied the marshal as he nodded towards the body and then added, 'He's the man who shot your pa in this very saloon.'

'Ryan didn't know that feller, Marshal,' said the barman and then added. 'That feller told me he was Ryan's long lost uncle and he was here to give him a surprise. He tricked me into pointing Ryan out to him when he came in.'

'Then I guess someone doesn't like you, young Ryan, because Mullen operated as a hired gun, or maybe he just saw you as a challenge after hearing about you getting the better of Rawlins.'

During his ride back home Ryan thought about the marshal identifying his pa's killer and he felt a strange sense that his life was about to change for the better. Now he had no doubts or loose ends to think about, except maybe what had happened to Ma. The marshal had told him about seeing the cheroot stubs near the barn, but explained that it could have been a drifter who had been intending to bed down in the barn. The drifter had probably fallen asleep while holding a lit cheroot and that's what started the fire. However, the marshal didn't really believe that was what happened and nor did Ryan.

During the weeks following his encounter with Mullen things had been quite normal. Ryan had gone into town and visited the saloon a few times, but there had been no incidents and he'd kept his drinking under control. He had even had a chin-wag with some of the Stratton boys, but they'd looked uncomfortable on one occasion when Kruger came into the saloon. One of the men told him that the two ranch-hands that had gone missing had never got on with Bryce.

Ryan hadn't missed a weekly visit to the cemetery to sit awhile close to his loved ones, spending most time near Ma's grave. He found that during his time there it brought him closer to them and it gave him some comfort.

He was riding back through town after his latest visit to the cemetery when he saw a familiar figure leaving Appleby's Store, carrying a newly purchased rifle. Ryan hadn't expected him to still be in town and he was tempted to pull up and talk to him, but the man didn't look to be in the talking mood and he was glowering at Ryan. He guessed his hostility was all to do with Melissa. Mark Kruger was still wearing his uniform like he had done on the night of the dance when he hadn't looked much happier than he did now. Ryan gave him a wave and turned his attention to the young woman who was about to mount the steps into the saloon. It was Janet and he touched the brim of his Stetson and nodded to her and she gave him a friendly smile. He hadn't spoken to her since the night she had nursed him after his brawl with ugly Vinny, but he would like to thank her properly the next time he was in town.

When Ryan turned to get a last look at Janet he saw Mark Kruger urging his horse towards him and kicking up the dust of Main Street as it galloped past him heading out of town.

SIXTEEN

Marshal Clancy's plans for a quiet afternoon catching up with some paperwork were ruined when a passerby came into his office all of a fluster and told him that a man was lying in the street and he was dead. The marshal told the man to calm down and hurried outside.

The marshal recognized the horse before he saw its owner lying face down on the ground beside it. The marshal had been joined by his deputy as he inspected the wounds and he told the deputy to go and get Doc Norris and tell him that Ryan Buchanan was either dead or in a very bad way.

Ryan felt drowsy as he focused on the two faces that seemed to be studying him. One face was pale and thin and the gold rimmed spectacles rested on the bridge of a long nose. He thought he was dreaming and then he caught a whiff of the disinfectant. Doc Norris was dabbing a bloodied pad on Ryan's chest. The other face was lined and rugged with a broad nose and the bushy beard was yellowed with tobacco stain and it belonged to Marshal Clancy.

'Welcome back, boy,' growled the marshal and then added, 'I thought the old doc had lost another of his patients and I guess the undertaker will be disappointed.'

Ryan tried to ease himself off the bed, but he winced at the pain in his shoulder where he had fallen from his horse, but it was the gaping wound in his chest that had caused the doc most concern when he'd been carried into his small surgery.

'I'll call back later, Doc, and ask this young feller how he got that bullet wound,' said the marshal.

Ryan had never really liked the taste of whiskey even though he'd drunk plenty of it to drown his sorrows, but the doc told him that without it he would be feeling more pain than any man could bear. The doc held the mug to Ryan's lips while he sipped the liquid that had been the downfall of many men, and before the doc had pulled the mug from his lips he was enjoying it. He would discover later that the doc had taken his last sip more than ten years ago. He had been drunk when he'd decided to amputate a man's leg that had been trapped under an overturned stagecoach. The doc had covered the man's legs with a blanket and had amputated the wrong leg.

Ryan was still feeling the pain from his wound when the marshal looked in the next day having been told by the doc on his previous visit that Ryan was a bit delirious and he wouldn't get much sense out of him.

Ryan's mouth felt dry and he sounded hoarse when he

replied to the marshal questions about the shooting.

'Not much to tell you, Marshal. I had come to town yesterday and so I decided to ride up to Burry's Point hoping to meet someone.'

'Would that someone happen to be Miss Melissa Stratton by any chance?'

'Now, Marshal, you know it wouldn't be a gentlemanly of me to reveal such information.'

'Getting shot hasn't stopped you being cheeky. So did you meet Melissa?'

Ryan apologized for joking with the marshal and then told him that Melissa was probably still away, but he'd hoped she might have returned earlier than planned. He'd waited for close on half an hour and then decided to head for town and call in at the saloon. He didn't tell the marshal that he'd hoped to see Janet.

As he approached the rocks on the trail that led to the Stratton ranch he was shot, but managed to stay in the saddle. He remembered thinking that he needed to get to Doc Norris. The marshal told him about the deputy discovering him on the ground outside the marshal's office and joked that he needed to train his horse better.

'It might just be a coincidence, but most of your troubles seemed to be linked to the Stratton ranch,' the marshal suggested and then continued, 'You must know that Major Stratton is not the sort of man to get on the wrong side of and it seems that you have. Firstly, by not selling your land to him and then by insisting on seeing his granddaughter even though he disapproves of you.'

Ryan wasn't surprised that the marshal might be suggesting that the major was behind the shooting. The marshal advised him to have a long think about what he wanted to do and whether it was worth staying in these parts.

'I'm not running away, Marshal. I made a silent promise to my ma when they lowered her into the ground that I would never sell the land to Major Stratton.'

'It's your life, son, but you could always find another buyer for your land or just leave it be until you come back one day. I'll ride out to the Stratton place later and make a few inquiries and just to make them aware that I suspect someone has it in for you.'

The doc had been listening and when the marshal left he asked Ryan an unexpected question.

'What side did your pa and uncle fight on during the war?'

'I don't honestly know, Doc, because they would never talk about it. Too many bad memories they'd said. Why do you ask?'

'I wasn't sure if you knew that they fought on the Confederate side and that might account for some of the animosity that Major Stratton might have had towards your family. Perhaps he just wanted the land, but maybe he wanted your family out of the territory.'

'I'm not following you, Doc. I would imagine that Major Stratton was on the Confederate side.'

The doc shook his head and then told Ryan that the major fought for the Union and he would never employ anyone who had served with the Confederates.

'Surely he wouldn't be bitter after all these years?' Ryan questioned the doc's reasoning.

'Most folks manage to forget the horrors of the war which I saw firsthand and before you ask I wasn't on either side. I joined a field hospital that treated men from both sides towards the end of the war.'

SEVENTEEN

It was two weeks after he'd returned home after being shot before Ryan felt strong enough to start working about the place. It was good to feel the warmth of the sun on his face and the freshness in the air. His gaze settled on the peaks of the mountain range in the distance and he was already planning on riding out to check on the herd later. The marshal had paid him a couple of visits and told him that his inquiries about who might have shot him had drawn a blank. The marshal had since decided that it was more likely to have been a horse thief who had hoped that Ryan would have fallen from his mount when he was shot. He had been tempted to mention to the marshal about seeing Mark Kruger in town the day before he was shot, but figured that if it had been Mark then he would have done it that same day.

Ryan had been having a slow walk near the cabin when he spotted the rider coming his way. He cursed for not buckling on his gun-belt, but it was too late now. Relief crossed Ryan's face when he recognized John Scully, one of his nearest neighbours.

113

'You still look mighty pale, Ryan. I would have called in earlier, but I only found out late yesterday about you being shot when I called in at the general store. John Appleby said that according to the doc it was pretty serious for a while on account of you losing so much blood.'

'I still feel a bit on the weak side, but I'm feeling much better today. In fact I was going to ride out to my herd later just to make sure they're all right.'

John Scully had been helpful since his uncle's death and Ryan was grateful when he offered to ride out with him to check on the herd.

John Scully owned the ranch next to the one that had belonged to Ryan's pa and Ryan planned to manage it again one day. The Scully ranch was closer to town and smaller than the Buchanans' ranch and Major Stratton had never shown any interest in buying the Scully place.

John Scully was just approaching his forty-sixth year; a thickset man with a shaggy beard and greying hair that looked as though it needed taming.

During the ride out to the herd Ryan and Scully discussed their plans to drive both their herds to market the following week. Ryan told him he would appreciate his advice when they got to the market; John Scully knew more about cattle than most men.

'They must have moved further towards the stream,' called out Ryan when they reached the spot where he expected the cattle to be grazing. Then he reminded himself how long it had been since he last checked on them.

Both men exchanged worried glances when their

search failed to locate the herd and when they did, Ryan gave an anguished cry. Most of them were dead or dying and the vultures continued with their scavenging, unperturbed for the moment that they were no longer alone. Ryan desperately scanned the herd looking for healthy animals, but none could be seen. The vultures waited until Ryan and Scully were close to them before they flew off with some carrying the torn flesh in their beaks while others had their claws clamped around what they had ripped from the stricken cattle.

'What could have happened to them, John?' Ryan asked with desperation in his voice. All that his Uncle Tom had worked for was lying strewn across the field and down into the stream where he could see some must have died in the water.

'It has to have been some deadly infection,' replied Scully and then added, 'but I remember seeing some animals die on a cattle drive once after they'd drunk some contaminated water.'

'You think they've been poisoned?' asked Ryan, growing angry at the thought that this was the work of some evil son of a bitch and if it was then it must be connected with Major Stratton.

'Stratton's boys have done this, haven't they, because no one else would be interested in trying to ruin me and drive me away?'

'You can't jump to conclusions, Ryan,' Scully cautioned and then advised, 'We need to get rid of these animals in case it's an infection and it gets spread by the buzzards, other birds or some foraging animals. I'll head back to my place and bring a team of horses with a cart and some materials. We need to put the dying cattle out of their misery and burn all the animals as soon as possible.'

Ryan was grateful once again for the older man's experience and when he asked what he could do, Scully told him to go and report it to the marshal and then hurry back.

Ryan was breathing heavily when he entered the marshal's office following his frantic ride to town.

Marshal Clancy looked up from polishing his marshal's badge and held it up as he spoke. 'This is only a piece of metal and I'm proud to wear it, but I sometimes think it's a "badge of trouble" and I hope you are not here to bring me some more.'

When the marshal took a closer look at Ryan his manner softened when he added, 'You don't look too good, young feller. Grab a seat while I pour you some coffee.'

When Ryan had finished explaining what had happened he then said he thought it was all down to Major Stratton. The marshal looked sympathetic and said it was a real shame, but then offered him the same advice as Scully had given about not jumping to conclusions without proof.

'Anyway, best we get out there and you can give Scully a hand while I have a look around and see if there are any clues as to what might have caused it. We'll call in at the doc's and see if he can ride out after us and offer an explanation. He's just as good with animals as he is with people.'

116

*

Marshal Clancy had ridden on many cattle drives before he became a lawman, but he'd never seen anything like the scene in front of him. Scully had already started killing the dying animals and suggested to Ryan that it would be best if they killed the few healthy looking animals that he'd located.

'But they look fine,' Ryan pleaded, eager to have at least have some animals to take to market.

'The animals could still have suffered in some way that hasn't shown up yet, but their meat could be poisoned,' Scully explained.

'Scully's right, Ryan. You just couldn't risk it because no one would ever buy cattle off you ever again if you sold them at the market and they ended up as diseased meat,' said the marshal sympathetically.

The three men had just finished killing the last of the healthy and dying animals when Doc Norris arrived on his old chestnut mare. The horse had travelled more miles than most horses during his visits to outlying home-steads to deliver babies or treat victims of fever and all manner of ailments. He rode past the carnage, surveying it as he went and headed for the stream.

Scully had used the cart horses to drag some of the animals to form a huge pile and had just started the first fire when the doc returned from his visit to the stream. He was holding a bottle. The doc slid down from his mount and was looking glum as he approached the trio and announced that he thought he'd found the problem.

117

'The stream's contaminated with something, but I'm no chemist, although you don't have to be one to see that this water isn't as it should be. If you were stupid enough to taste it you would realize it isn't right.'

Ryan looked at the cloudy liquid in the bottle and than queried something with the doc. 'But I thought animals had an instinct for things they shouldn't eat or drink, just by smelling them.'

'That's generally true, young Ryan, but your poor cattle might have been slowly poisoned when the solution was weaker than it is now.'

The marshal told Ryan that he would have to put up some warning notices even though the stream was on his land. There was further bad news for Ryan when the older men explained to him that it would mean that no cattle could use the stream until the pollution had been cleared and that that could take a very long time. The doc recalled cases near mining areas that had been polluted by deposits from the mine getting into the water stream, but that couldn't have happened here. Scully had suggested that it might have been a case of a dead animal lying in the water and its decaying carcass being the cause of the pollution. The marshal, like Ryan, wondered if the pollution might have been manmade, but he kept his thoughts to himself. There was no point in adding to Ryan's grief without there being some evidence.

It took Ryan and Scully, helped by one of Scully's temporary cowhands three days to burn the carcasses and bury the remains. Ryan knew that if ever he raised cattle again then it would likely be on his pa's old land on the adjoining ranch. He wouldn't be able to risk having cattle graze on what was now a mass burial ground for the cattle that were meant to be his future.

During the weeks that followed the discovery of his poisoned cattle, Ryan became convinced that the pollution was the work of Major Stratton. The marshal had spoken about needing proof and he knew that short of torturing Stratton he had to accept that he would never get the evidence he needed. The Major Strattons of this world didn't do their own dirty work, but relied upon men like Karl Kruger to do it for them. Doc Norris had told Ryan that Kruger had served under the major towards the end of the war and Kruger was as loyal as they came.

Ryan had gone over to John Scully's to ask if he could work for him to tide him over, but Scully told him that there wasn't enough work for an extra man. He knew that Scully would have helped him if he could. So he returned home, disappointed, but at least it had decided things for him and he planned to leave the following day. He would miss the company of Scully who had partly replaced his Uncle Tom and given him lots of advice. He had no real plans except to see a bit of life and try to forget Major Stratton's evil-doing. It wouldn't be easy because he would always wonder if he was behind the death of his beloved Ma.

He'd packed a few faded photographs and the pen that Ma had bought him when he'd started school, even though it was broken. He'd double checked that there was nothing else of any value and then he remembered the chest that had been kept under Ma and Uncle Tom's bed. Ma had called it her box of 'little treasures' and Uncle Tom had playfully accused her of hoarding junk.

Ryan was excited and curious as he prepared to open the chest. He smiled when he saw the first wooden pistol that his pa had carved out for him and the catapult that his Uncle Tom had made him. There was a collection of buttons that Ryan remembered being on some of the clothes he'd worn as a boy. The last item he pulled from the bottom of the chest was a collection of photographs, some of which were badly faded. He guessed most of them were family, but only a few had names on the back. When he turned over the last photograph of four men in uniform and read the names on the back he was puzzled for a moment. When the significance of the names dawned on him he decided that if he was leaving tomorrow it would be after he had paid Major Stratton a visit.

EIGHTEEN

Ryan pulled up his mount when he saw the signpost to the Stratton ranch and was thinking it had been a big mistake to come here while he was so full of anger, but there was no turning back now. He hoped that when he left here he could pay a visit to the family graves and feel that his family were truly laid to rest and avenged for what had happened to them. Then he could get on with his life and put the misery of recent events behind him.

He didn't recognize the rider who was approaching until he was close enough to see that he had a rifle straddled across his horse's saddle. He had only ever seen Mark Kruger in uniform recently and not in the working clothes he now donned.

'Are you going hunting, buddy?' Ryan asked as he glanced at the rifle. Kruger appeared nervous, surprised by the unexpected meeting with the man he had grown to hate and he stuttered as he explained that he was going to do some shooting practice.

'I thought you would have gone back to your barracks by now,' Ryan said, grateful for the delay in his own mission at the Stratton ranch.

'I may not be going back if things work out with me and Melissa,' replied Kruger in a more confident tone.

'I didn't know you and Melissa were serious. I thought you were more like brother and sister. Is Melissa back home?'

'No,' Kruger snapped and then added. 'You caused trouble between her and her grandfather and if you have any feelings for Melissa then you'll leave her be when she comes home.'

'It's up to Melissa and it's none of your business if she wants to see me, but things might be different after today because I'm on my way to see her grandpa now. You might be in for a surprise later when you hear a few home truths about your pa.'

Kruger looked taken aback and waited for Ryan to explain what he meant. Ryan just heeled his horse forward, but glanced back after he had ridden no more than a dozen strides. Kruger hadn't moved and both his hands were holding the rifle. Ryan pulled his mount up and turned to face Kruger, then waited until he turned his horse and rode off at a gallop.

Mark Kruger was still smarting from being on the receiving end of his pa's anger just before his meeting with Ryan. They had argued over his failure to win over the affections of Melissa Stratton and let a simple cowboy like Ryan Buchanan muscle his way in. Karl Kruger had reminded his son of the advantages he had been given by the generosity of Major Stratton which had allowed him to have a fine education and a career in the military. Karl Kruger was convinced that the major wanted Mark and

Melissa to get married one day and that is exactly what he wanted too. He had left Mark in no doubt that his son should be prepared to do whatever it took to win over Melissa's affection even if it meant making sure that Ryan Buchanan didn't mess things up. Mark had heard about someone shooting Ryan and he wondered if that had anything to do with his pa. He had been on the verge of telling his pa about not being able to return to the military academy, but perhaps now he really could make the excuse of needing to stay at home and spend more time with Melissa.

Mark had mulled over his options and thinking how he could sort things out with his pa. He'd finally decided what he was going to do and put an end to his troubles.

Ryan faltered when he approached the house and saw the palomino tied to the hitch rail near the stables. It was Melissa's horse and he figured that someone must have been exercising it. He wondered what she would think of him when all this was over and if she would want to see him again.

He had gone over in his mind how he would handle the confrontation and he tried to calm himself as he tied the reins of his horse to the hitch rail near the house. He hadn't considered the possibility that the major may not even be at home, but when he saw the well dressed man leaving the house he guessed he had been there to do some business with the major. The man nodded to him, perhaps assuming that he was a ranch-hand. This was no time for niceties, waiting to be invited in, so he turned the handle on the large front door and then entered the spacious hallway. He'd never been in anything so grand and he was on the point of trying to decide which of the many doors he should go through when he heard a man clearing his throat in the room opposite.

The major had just poured a large whiskey and was about to take a puff on the half smoked fat cigar when he looked up and saw Ryan.

'What are you doing here and how dare you walk in uninvited!' the major growled at him, clearly shocked by such an ill mannered intrusion by a young man he had hoped he would never see again.

'Major. I'm here to ask you a few questions about your determination to get rid of my family which had nothing to do with you wanting our land.'

'You're talking in riddles,' the major replied as his face reddened with anger.

'You knew that my uncle and pa fought in the war on the side of General Montrose which was on the opposite side that you claim to have fought on.'

'Yes, I did, but where is all this leading?' the major asked, showing his irritation.

'You arranged for a hired gun to kill my pa and then hired him again to try and kill me. Your men set fire to the barn in which my ma died. Then you tried to drive me out by having your men poison the stream on my land.'

'I'm an ex soldier and rancher and I don't hire killers. I was shocked when I heard the news about the fire, but it was probably just an accident. I admit I didn't like your pa or uncle very much, but I had nothing to do with their deaths or any of the other things you claim.'

'You're an impostor, Major and so is Karl Kruger. You both fought on the same side as my pa and Uncle Tom and that's why you wanted them to leave here in case they revealed the truth about you.'

'Don't talk nonsense and leave now before I have you dragged off my land.'

'Your game's up, Major and here's the proof.'

Ryan had removed the faded photograph from his pocket and placed it on the major's desk.

The major picked up the photograph of four soldiers in Confederate uniform. One of them was wearing an officer's uniform and the area around his face had been damaged by a stain.

'Read the names on the back,' Ryan said in a tone that was more of an order than a request.

Ryan watched the major's expression change when he looked at the back of the photograph and the faded writing which read: Jack Buchanan, Tom Buchanan, Captain Stratton, Lon Leeson (Karl Kruger).

Ryan saw the major look over Ryan's shoulder, but he realized too late that someone was behind him and he felt a pistol being jabbed into his neck followed by the sound of the hammer being drawn back.

'I heard what the kid said, Major, and it sounds as though he's fired up with liquor, or just plain crazy. What shall I do with him?'

Kruger had pulled Ryan's gun from its holster and pushed it inside his own gun-belt. He had always admired the gun and he wouldn't be returning it.

'Escort him off my land and make sure that he never returns.'

'I'll be back, Major, and I'll bring the marshal next time. He'll believe me when I tell him that you are both a couple of impostors. Is that why you always acted as though you hated anyone who'd fought on the Confederate side? Why did you pretend to be on the Union side?'

'You best leave right now, kid, while you can still walk,' Kruger ordered and then pushed Ryan towards the door of the study. If they had turned around they would have seen the major studying the photograph through tear-filled eyes.

Kruger continued to prod Ryan forward until they were out of the house and then he ordered him to mount his horse which was tethered alongside his own.

'Don't try anything stupid, kid, because I'll be riding right behind you.'

Ryan looked towards the bunkhouse and it brought back a memory which prompted him to ask Kruger a question.

'Was it you who killed Bryce on the night of the barn dance and tried to put the blame on me?'

Kruger laughed before he replied, 'You got away with that one, kid and you shouldn't have pushed your luck by coming here.'

Kruger's reply hadn't been what Ryan had expected it would be. He'd hoped that Kruger might have admitted what happened because Ryan was certain that Kruger intended to kill him once they were well away from the ranch house and in no danger of being seen.

'What was on that photograph?' Kruger asked.

'It shows you and the major in Confederate uniform

standing with my pa and uncle. You must have used the name Lon Leeson then and it was taken when Stratton was a captain.'

Kruger looked worried when he said, 'You've got this all wrong, kid, and you should have kept your wild ideas to yourself, but I don't suppose it matters now. You've messed things up for me and signed your own death warrant. Now move forward so I can keep you covered.'

They had just reached some small hills and were well clear of the ranch when a shot rang out and Ryan's first thought was that Kruger had shot him in the back even though he hadn't felt the impact of a bullet. When Ryan turned in his saddle he expected to see Kruger ready to finish him off, but then he saw Kruger lying close to some small rocks and one side of his face was covered in blood. A second shot rang out and the bullet thudded into the ground near Ryan, causing his horse to rear up. He quickly brought the horse under control before he dismounted and then knelt beside the unconscious Kruger. There was more blood on the rock that Kruger's head had struck when he'd fallen from his horse. Ryan pulled his own pistol from Kruger's belt and scanned the rocks some distance away, waiting for the next shot to ring out.

Kruger's horse had returned to stand in front of where Ryan was crouched, offering some protection from one direction, but blocking his view, until it walked off and then Ryan saw a rider who was galloping towards him. Ryan directed his pistol towards the rider, but was shocked when the horse drew closer. It was a horse he had seen many times and it was being ridden by Melissa Stratton.

Ryan stood up, forgetting the danger from whoever fired the shots, not able to believe that it could have been Melissa.

'What have you done? I heard the shots,' she screeched after she'd dismounted and seen the blood on Kruger.

'I haven't done anything, Melissa. Someone fired at us and Kruger fell from his horse. I don't think he was hit and must have struck his head on the rock. I went to see the major and Kruger was making sure that I left. I thought you were still away.'

Melissa told him that she had only returned yesterday and then asked him why he had visited her grandfather. When Ryan explained that he thought her grandfather was involved in the things that had happened to his family, including the death of his own ma, Melissa reacted angrily.

'I thought I knew you better,' Melissa snapped. 'How could you think that he would be involved in those horrible things that happened to you and your family? The captain on that photograph must have been my father who fought on the opposite side to Grandfather. Suggesting he is some kind of an impostor is just plain stupid. Kruger must have changed sides as well as his name. I am sure that Grandfather didn't know that Kruger once fought on the opposite side to him.'

Melissa told Ryan that she was going to ride back to the ranch to get some help for Kruger and made it clear that she never wanted to see him again. She didn't seem interested in his apology and admission that he might have got it all wrong. She was tearful when she galloped off after Ryan had told her that Kruger was beyond help because he was dead.

Ryan watched Melissa ride off and was no longer thinking that he might be in danger if the gunman was still out there waiting to take another shot. Ryan had some serious thinking to do, but first he needed to report what had happened to the marshal.

Only a handful of people attended Karl Kruger's funeral and neither his son, nor Mayor Stratton was amongst them. The major felt only bitterness towards the man who had fooled him for so many years and risked ruining the major's reputation by his personal vendetta against the Buchanans.

Ryan regretted ruining his relationship with Melissa, but he guessed it was very likely that she would have been leaving for good at some point. He talked things through with the marshal and they agreed that Kruger was the one who had the real motive for getting the Buchanan family out of the area and the major was innocent.

Ryan decided to put his plans to leave on hold and visited his nearest neighbour John Scully on his way to town and told him that he was staying on at his ranch. Unlike the marshal, Scully wasn't convinced that the major hadn't been involved with at least some of the incidents that had caused misery for the Buchanan family. Scully declined Ryan's invitation to join him in the saloon because he hadn't drunk hard liquor since his wife had left him nearly five years ago. Some say that his wife left him because she just couldn't cope any more with his drinking which he had taken up to cope with the appalling injuries he had suffered in the war. Scully had lived alone since his wife's departure apart from the occasional hired help who stayed in the small bunkhouse.

Jim Peters was mopping up some spilt beer off the bar and his eyes drifted towards Ryan's belt buckle when he saw him approaching. He was surprised to see that Ryan wasn't carrying his much talked about pistol and was unarmed.

'What will it be, young Ryan?' the barman asked and Ryan ordered his usual beer.

'You seem in a cheerful mood, Ryan and I hope that means no brawling tonight. That group over there are beginning to get a bit rowdy, so do me a favour and try and stay clear of them.'

Ryan's promise that he wouldn't be staying long enough to get too drunk didn't materialize, although he remained in a good mood. He enjoyed some banter with Vicky, but he staggered a little when he made his way out of the saloon. He was surprised to see that it was already dark and reminded himself to ride nice and slow on his way home.

'What are you smiling at?' Ryan asked when his foot missed the stirrup at the first attempt. It was Ryan who was smiling when the ginger and white stray dog who he had addressed his question to cocked its head on one side.

'I guess all your girlfriends have bedded down for the night and you are out scrounging for some leftover grub.'

Ryan finally mounted his horse and bid the dog good-night as he heeled his horse forward, but rode slowly down Main Street. He was still smiling when he reached the edge of town and heeled his horse into a slow trot, unaware that he was being followed.

Ryan had flopped onto his bed fully clothed when he'd arrived home and was still wearing his Stetson when he woke up. The room was dark and his thoughts were muddled because he usually only awakened when he was ready to get up. His mouth was parched and he thought about getting up to have a drink of water, but he decided to snuggle down again and get back to sleep. Then the barking started again. It was the barking that had woken him, but he hadn't realized it.

Ryan groaned when he remembered the stray mutt that had followed him home and he had brought into the cabin, but he was soon laughing as the ginger and white mongrel licked his face. He gently pushed the animal away and then he sniffed, but it wasn't the smelly dog that concerned him, but the smoke that had drifted into his nostrils making him leap from his bed. The dog cowered away thinking that his new master was angry with him. Ryan dashed into the other room and cursed when he saw the flames that had just flared up around the door of the cabin. He hadn't bothered to light a lamp when he returned last night so he was puzzled how the fire could have flared. Then he realized that it had been started outside the cabin and it must have been started deliberately.

Ryan used a chair to smash the only window in the

cabin even though it was too small to escape through. His action had been a big mistake and the flames erupted even further and he couldn't let the dog escape though the window like he'd planned. The dog was barking furiously as Ryan considered running though the flame-filled doorway holding the dog, but faltered when he saw that a section of the roof and side walls were now ablaze.

Ryan forced open his eyelids. He blinked, hoping to ease the smarting sensation he felt in his eyes. He had vague memories of someone talking to him as they rode alongside him. He gave a weak smile when the dog placed its paws on the side of the bed. He remembered pushing the dog though the gap in the cabin roof just before part of the roof came crashing down.

'How are you feeling, young man, if that don't sound like a dumb question?' asked Doc Norris as he surveyed Ryan's blackened and burnt face.

'Not too good, Doc and I'm wondering how I ended up here.'

The doc explained that Judd Kenley found him near Ryan's burnt out cabin and rode into town with Ryan strapped to his own horse. The doc didn't know how old Judd had managed to get him up on the horse, but if he hadn't passed by when he did during the early morning then Ryan would likely be dead.

'Your friend there got off with just a lightly singed back. He followed you and Judd all the way here. Judd said that when he found you the dog was licking the wounds on your face. Talking of finding, the marshal was in here earlier asking how you were doing and he was a bit upset because he's lost his marshal's badge.'

'Am I going to be OK, Doc?' Ryan asked.

'You're young and strong, Ryan, and most of your wounds will heal quickly and luckily your face didn't suffer too much. I'm afraid you suffered some injuries that might never fully heal, especially those to your hands, but we'll have to wait and see.'

Ryan finally got the all clear from the doc and prepared to make the journey to the old cabin where he'd lived before his pa died. Judd Kenley had spent the past week living there and preparing the place for Ryan to return to.

'I'm going to miss having that old dog around,' said the doc as he helped Ryan walk to the hitch rail outside the surgery. Judd had brought Ryan's sorrel from the livery ready for the ride home and it was alongside his horse.

Ryan thanked the doc and told him that he would follow the instructions he had given him and call in next week and have his dressings checked over.

The doc had a concerned expression as he watched Ryan's horse being led behind the old trapper's with the dog running alongside as they made their way down Main Street. He wondered if Ryan would ever be able to hold a horse's reins in the normal way and he hoped that Ryan had the strength of character to cope. Life was never going to be quite the same for the young man.

NINETEEN

Ryan had been grateful to Judd Kenley, not just for saving his life, but for the help he'd given him in settling into his new home, but now he would have to start coping on his own.

'I could stay a few days longer before I go and lay my traps up at Egremore Lake,' said Kenley, ending with his usual whistle on account of his missing teeth.

'I'll be just fine, Mr Kenley, and I owe you at least a good night's drinking in the saloon when you get back.'

Kenley had given up trying to get Ryan to call him by his first name, but he was pleased that the youngster showed him respect the way he did.

Judd pulled on the leather straps of his horse's saddle, checked it was in position and then secured his bedroll and water containers. He'd told Ryan that he still missed his old mule that had died a month ago from old age and he'd decided to replace him with a horse. The buckskin hadn't cost him much on account of its age, and Judd had figured that the horse would outlive him and he got himself a bargain.

Judd mounted the buckskin with a grunt and told Ryan that he would look forward to that beer and that Ryan needed to follow the doc's advice and not try to rush things.

'I'll bring a little present for your faithful friend there to chew on,' Judd promised as he nodded towards the dog sat beside Ryan.

'He'd appreciate that. Go easy, Mr Kenley and thanks again for all your help.'

Judd waved his hand and heeled his horse forward, hoping that the young feller he'd become fond of was going to be all right on his own. He had experienced his own share of misery and seen some loved ones die before their time. Ryan had suffered so much grief in his young life and it would have been tough for anyone to handle.

Ryan waited until he saw Judd stop some distance from the cabin and turn around to give Ryan a final wave.

'Right, you old scrounger,' Ryan said addressing the dog. 'I think I ought to give you a name. What do you think of Toby?'

The dog cocked its head like it frequently did and Ryan laughed before he said, 'You didn't bark your objection, so I guess, Toby, it is.'

Judd had saddled Ryan's horse before he left because Ryan planned to go and look over the burnt out cabin. He struggled to mount the horse and then he fumbled with the reins before he settled for holding them with just his left hand that had suffered far less damage than the other one.

'Come on then, Toby,' he called to the dog after he'd

heeled his horse forward. The dog had been eagerly waiting for the order and was soon scurrying after Ryan's horse.

Ryan was having some regrets when the destroyed cabin came into view and was thinking that it might have been better to have remembered it as it was in happier times. Only the small shed remained untouched by the two fires that had destroyed the work of his uncle and his pa who had constructed the cabins and barns on both their ranches.

He painstakingly sifted through the ruins of the cabin with a small stick held in his least damaged hand. His hopes of finding some memento that might have survived were raised when he saw the picture frame that Ma had given him on his birthday. It had been scorched and when he turned it over nothing remained of the portrait of Ma and his uncle. He intended to ask Judd if he could sketch another portrait of them from memory.

He made his way towards his horse ready to leave and perhaps never to return and was surprised that the newly christened Toby wasn't waiting for him. Then he spotted the dog some distance away, but it was soon heading towards him.

'What have you got there?' Ryan called out as the dog came closer holding something it its mouth.

The dog dropped the object close to Ryan's feet as though it was a trophy gift for his master. Ryan had seen the metal object many times before, but he was puzzled as to why it should be on his land and tried to dismiss the thought that was going though his mind because it didn't make sense. He needed to find out if the man who had lost it had tried to burn him alive and perhaps been responsible for other things that had happened since his eighteenth birthday.

Ryan felt his anger grow as he mounted his sorrel. He planned to head home to pick up his pistol and then he was going to find Marshal Clancy!

TWENTY

Ryan stood outside the cemetery he had visited every Sunday since Ma had been buried there except when he was being treated in the doc's surgery. During one of his visits he had seen the man he was now waiting to confront, but Ryan had never known whose grave it was the man attended to until earlier today. He was still finding it hard to believe that he could have been so evil and carried so much hate for such a long time.

The man he had trusted and thanked for his help was walking towards him and now there was no doubt he was the one who had tried to burn him alive as he'd slept in his cabin. Ryan had felt himself tense and his left hand reached towards the pistol he had tucked in his belt just as Marshal Clancy had stepped from behind the bushes.

The man saw them and put his hand behind his back, but it was a futile attempt that was about to be exposed when Marshal Clancy addressed him.

'I believe this is yours, Scully?' the marshal declared as he held up the metal hook.

Scully looked surprised and as nervous as hell and

didn't look Ryan in the eye as he explained how he had lost the metal hook that replaced the hand he'd lost in the war.

'When did you last visit Tom and Meg's place?' the marshal asked.

'What's all this about, Marshal? I lost the hook out near the lake like I said and if it was found near where the fire was then someone must have taken it there.'

'You're lying, Scully,' the marshal accused and then added, 'It was you who set fire to the cabin while Ryan was asleep inside. John Appleby told me that you ordered a chemical from him a while ago, but he couldn't remember what excuse you gave for needing it. You used that chemical to poison the stream and it was you who set fire to the barn that poor Meg died in. You must have been chain smoking those cheroots you are so fond of whose stubs you left behind while you waited to do your evil work. Did you really hate the Buchanan family that much because of what happened to your brother even though he deserved it?'

The mention of his brother made Scully's face contort with rage and he gave up any pretence as he admitted hating the family.

'I didn't intend Meg to die like that. It was meant to frighten her and I didn't expect her to go to the barn. I just wanted Ryan to leave the ranch and I thought he would move on after I had contaminated the stream. I couldn't stand being reminded of what his family did to my brother with their lies. His gun-happy pa threatened to shoot an innocent man. He would have done as well if the mob hadn't burnt him alive in his cabin because he

139

was too frightened to come out.'

Ryan had managed to control himself as he'd listened, but he stepped forward and raised his own damaged hand ready to smash it into Scully's face, but was held back by the marshal.

'Leave it, Ryan. This poor excuse for a man is going to face a hanging.'

The marshal drew his pistol and ordered Scully to start walking into town and his office.

Ryan told the marshal that he was going to visit his family's graves, but would call in at his office before he left town.

Ryan had been tempted to confront Scully when his dog had found the distinctive metal hook that must have fallen to the ground after Scully had set fire to the cabin. Ryan had visited the marshal and told him about the find and how it didn't make sense that Scully could be implicated in the fire because he had been so helpful to Ryan. The marshal had been surprised that Ryan had not been aware of the 'history' between the two families. The marshal told Ryan that Scully's brother, Doug, had raped Ryan's mother while his pa and Uncle Tom were on a cattle drive. When Jack Buchanan returned home he discovered that his wife had drowned herself in the lake because of the shame. He went looking for Doug Scully, but word had already spread and when Doug Scully refused to come out and face Jack the mob started the fire. John Scully refused to accept that his brother was guilty and believed that Ryan's mother had flirted with his brother because she was missing her man. During the past few years it had appeared that John Scully had put his brother's death behind him, and had become friendly with Ryan's uncle, but now it seemed it was just an act. He had fooled Ryan with his offer to help him after his uncle had died when all the time he must have been planning to continue his revenge.

Ryan spent longer than usual beside the graves after the confrontation with Scully and when he finally arrived at the marshal's office he received some more shocking revelations. The marshal told him that Scully had just seemed to go berserk when he was locked up in the cell and said that what he'd done to the Buchanans was worth hanging for.

'The sick son of a bitch said that he hired Mullen to kill your pa and then again when Mullen tried to kill you in the saloon.'

'How could someone build up all that hate even if his brother had been innocent?' Ryan asked.

'I think it might also have something to do what happened to him in the war, losing his hand the way he did and having three fingers missing off the remaining hand. There's something else that will come as a surprise to you, young Ryan.'

'I think I'm past being surprised by anything, Marshal. What is it?'

'Scully claims that he was the one who shot you when you were up near the Stratton ranch. It seems that I was wrong about it being a horse thief.'

'But how could he fire a gun with those fingers missing on his hand?' asked Ryan who had been wrong about not being surprised any more!

'Apparently he rigged up something on his rifle that

let him pull the trigger and I don't think he's lying. He seemed to just want to boast about what he'd done to your family.'

Ryan gave a deep sigh as the significance sunk in and he realized that he had got it all wrong, first about Major Stratton and then Kruger. He admitted to the marshal that he had been a fool to accuse the major like he did.

'I could have told you that the major's military background was genuine and that he fought on the Union side, but I didn't know about his son or about Kruger switching sides. I guess you messed things up with his granddaughter, but there is still a mystery about who killed Bryce and who fired the shot that caused Kruger to fall from his horse and smash his brains out on a rock.'

Ryan asked the marshal if he thought Scully might have fired the shots the day that Kruger fell from his horse and the marshal told him that he had quizzed Scully about it and he denied doing it.

'I still think that it was Mark who tried to kill me that day and he must have been devastated that he had caused his own pa's death.'

'You could be right,' the marshal agreed. 'It would explain why he's gone missing and didn't attend Karl Kruger's funeral, but we will never know unless he shows up again. Anyway, young feller, I need to get on with some paperwork. You did the right thing coming to see me when you found that hook. Perhaps that dog of yours can find my lost marshal's badge!'

Ryan left the marshal's office and planned to visit Appleby's store before heading home. He had a lot of thinking to do and a lot of regretting concerning how

things had ended with Melissa. He knew that he would-
n't be able to rest easy until there was some news about
Mark Kruger because if he was right about him then
Mark might still have some unfinished business with
Ryan.

TWENTY-ONE

Three weeks after Scully's arrest Ryan was on the way back from the canyon when he spotted a horse. There was a familiar figure standing beside it. For a moment he thought it best to ride on, but decided he would regret it so he pulled up alongside.

'Has that fine horse of yours picked up another stone,' he asked and was surprised when she smiled.

'The truth is I have been waiting to see you,' replied Melissa.

'I'm sorry for those things I said to your grandfather and I'd like to tell him to his face how sorry I am, but I guess he wouldn't be interested even if I ever got close enough to speak to him.'

'I don't think you really know my grandfather. He's heard what you have been through and he's sorry for you. We all are, especially after what happened to you in the fire. It must have been horrible.'

She asked him how he was coping with the problems to his hands and he tried to sound positive and didn't reveal his frustration at not being able to do the simplest of things. He's stopped carrying a gun because at present it was so difficult to pull the trigger, so there didn't seem any point. Before they parted he agreed to visit the Stratton ranch the following morning and speak to her grandfather after she'd told him that he would be welcome.

Ryan rode off, his mood lifted by his meeting with Melissa and when he'd gripped the reins firmly with his left hand he'd felt some movement in his fingers that he hadn't experienced before. He planned to visit Appleby's store soon and buy a new left handed holster and then he would try some practice shooting with his left hand.

Ryan's visit to see Major Stratton went as well as he could have hoped for, even though it wasn't quite as friendly as Melissa had suggested it would be. The major accepted his apology and he had seemed genuine when he expressed his sympathy for Ryan's recent misfortune, but he had hinted that Melissa was best suited to the sophistication of city life. Ryan had been a bit taken aback when the major had asked him who he thought had killed Bryce on the night of Melissa's barn dance. It was something that was often in Ryan's thoughts, but he told the major that the only people who might be able to solve the mystery were the two men who had blamed him.

When he left the Stratton house a smiling Melissa was stroking and patting his horse and had obviously been waiting for him.

'So did he invite you back for Sunday tea?' she asked and laughed.

'Not this Sunday, but he was fine and let me off lightly considering I was so wrong when I accused him. I still don't think he approves of us being friends and probably thinks you should only mix with city dudes.'

'I pick my own horses and I pick my own friends and grandfather will have to get used to that. So what will you do when your hand gets better?'

Ryan looked down at his damaged hand and gave a rueful smile before he replied. 'I don't have many options, but I think I might try breeding horses using this fine horse of mine as the stud. My uncle Tom won him in a game of cards when he was at a cattle market in Tasmont and he must have come from some fine stock.'

Melissa told him that she had an idea and might be able to help, but she wouldn't tell him what it was in case he was disappointed if it didn't come off. Then she told him some bad news which was that she would be leaving again next week to visit her aunt back East.

The day before Melissa was due to travel to her aunt's she visited Ryan and delivered him some surprising and good news. Her grandfather had agreed to provide two mares when they were in season and would allow Ryan to keep them until he built up his breeding stock.

Ryan hugged her to offer his thanks and paused before he kissed her, unsure how she would respond, but he needn't have worried and it was some time before she eased herself free.

'I don't think Grandfather would have offered the animals had he realized that this would have been the outcome of me breaking the news to you,' Melissa said

146

with a smile.

Ryan's thoughts were not on his business or anything else other than Melissa when he asked her if she really had to leave.

'I promised Aunt Muriel and she would be so disappointed. She will have made big plans for my visit and arranged for my friends to come and see me and I will be seeing Andrew. I should have told you about Andrew.'

'I guess he's one of those city dudes your grandfather mentioned and must be your boyfriend.'

Melissa replied that Andrew was both and that she had better be going because she had lots of packing to do.

Ryan held the reins of Melissa's horse as she mounted it. She wished him luck with his new venture, but before she rode off Ryan had a question about something that still bothered him.

'On the night that Bryce was killed, did I really spend time with you like you told the marshal? I must have taken a real whack on the head and I still don't remember some of the things that happened that night.'

'You really don't remember, do you? So perhaps it's best that you don't.'

Melissa gave that teasing smile that she often did and then heeled her horse into action leaving behind a very confused and disappointed Ryan.

TWENTY-TWO

Ryan had spent most of the three weeks since Melissa had left struggling to build a corral for what he hoped would be used by the breeding stock and then by new arrivals that would hopefully follow.

He had made his weekly visit to the cemetery yesterday and seen Marshal Clancy on his way out of town. The marshal told him that Scully's trial would start on Thursday and that Charles Maddison, the town's only lawyer, wanted Ryan to meet him at the marshal's office tomorrow. The marshal didn't have any details except to say that it had nothing to do with the trial.

So when Ryan entered the marshal's office for the appointment the following day he was curious to find out what it was all about.

Charles Maddison was already seated and he stood up before offering his hand to Ryan and appeared embarrassed when Ryan offered him his less damaged left hand.

Charles Maddison was fifty-five years old, tall and thin and always wore a black suit giving the impression he was in mourning for someone. Ryan had met him before when he had visited their ranch to make an offer on behalf of Major Stratton and he had yet to see Maddison smile. Ryan guessed this was about the ranch, but was puzzled why the meeting was being held in the marshal's office.

'I'm not selling any land, Mr Maddison.'

Ryan's comment did actually make a faint smile appear on the legal man's face before he replied, 'I am here to represent Mr Scully and it is not about you selling any land. On the contrary, it is just the opposite in fact, and I will now explain it to you.'

As Maddison outlined the reasons why the meeting had been called, Ryan caught the eye of the marshal a few times and saw him look skywards, no doubt because of the long winded legal jargon. Maddison could have explained it all in a few short sentences, but it would still have left Ryan uncertain as to what to say when he was asked what he thought of the proposal.

Ryan gave a deep sigh and shook his head before he replied that he didn't want anything from the man who had reaped such havoc on him and his family. The marshal had anticipated Ryan's dismissive response and was primed to offer him some advice.

'For what it's worth, Ryan, I think Scully knows that he did some evil things and he feels so much guilt because I suspect he now finally accepts that his brother was guilty. He's going to hang and so this isn't a gesture that will give him any benefit, except maybe a slight easing of his conscience.'

'I just feel it would be like accepting blood money,'

Ryan replied and he wasn't prepared for what Maddison was about to reveal.

'The decision is yours, Mr Buchanan, but if you turn down the offer of Mr Scully's property then it will be given to Major Stratton for free. I should also tell you that my client wants you to have a sum of just over one thousand dollars which is deposited in the bank here in town.'

Ryan was in turmoil and he asked if there were any conditions attached and would he be expected to see John Scully, because he wouldn't do that.

Maddison told him that there were no conditions and that his client had told him that he couldn't face Ryan. He just wanted him to know how sorry he was.

Ryan reluctantly agreed to accept what he had been offered, but there was no feeling of excitement when he signed the document that was witnessed by the marshal. Maddison would deliver him a copy of all the legal documents in a few days and make arrangements for withdrawing the money from the bank. The marshal gave a cynical smile when Maddison informed Ryan that there would be a charge for his services that would need to be deducted before Ryan could access the money held in the bank.

Ryan left the marshal's office and was tempted to visit the saloon, but his emotions were still confused and he was wondering if he had done the right thing in accepting the property and money.

Marshal Clancy didn't like wearing formal attire, but he guessed there was no way of avoiding it today. Judge

Henry Bloomfield was a stickler for formalities and would have cast a disapproving eye if the marshal wasn't suitably dressed for Scully's murder trial which was due to start at 10 o'clock. The marshal had remembered last year when the judge had adjourned a case because the clerk of the court had attended court in a fancy waistcoat. The clerk had been sent home and returned in more sober attire looking shamefaced.

The marshal had no sympathy for John Scully even though he had shown real remorse in recent days. The man had obviously been unbalanced by the war and was not naturally evil like some men the marshal had come across, but there could be no excuse for the things that he'd done.

The marshal did a careful trim of his beard and brushed his suit for the third time before he left his tiny cabin at the end of Main Street and set off to his office.

There was a bustle about the place and more people on the street than usual, including the morbid ones who relished the thought of a hanging.

Deputy Ty Milligan was thumbing his way though a book on locomotives and jumped when the marshal entered the office and asked if Scully had eaten his breakfast and inquired after his mood.

'He's fine, Marshal, and spoke more to me this morning than all the time he's been locked up. He even smiled a lot and told me that the court would be in for a big surprise later. I think he's got something up his sleeve if you ask me.'

'You're still too gullible, Deputy. That's just his way of coping with things. It would have been all nervous talk like I've seen others do. I've known men appear as brave as hell and then peed in their pants as soon as they were sentenced to a hanging. Anyway, you had better go and fetch him and we'll take him over to the courthouse nice and early. We don't want to upset the judge by being late.'

The marshal sat down at his desk and perused some of the notes he'd made to remind himself of the various events that he'd investigated, including the two fires and the poisoned stream.

'Time we were moving the prisoner,' the marshal shouted out to his deputy who had gone into the cell area.

When his deputy didn't reply for the second time of asking the marshal moved quickly towards the cells, drawing his pistol as he went.

Deputy Milligan was in a state of shock as he stared into the cell and he didn't respond when the marshal said, 'Jesus,' and then pulled the deputy away and ordered him to leave the cells, fearing that he was about to puke. Scully had been right about the court being in for a surprise because it would be opened and closed with a short statement from the judge. John Scully was lying in a large pool of his own blood. The metal hook that he had dropped on the night he set fire to Ryan's cabin had been used to rip open his own throat and was still lodged in the gaping wound. The marshal would discover later that he had asked for it when the deputy had delivered his breakfast and said that he would feel more comfortable in court if he had it on.

TWENTY-THREE

Ryan had felt no emotion when he had learned of John Scully's death. He had worked hard in setting up his stud farm despite the handicap of having only the use of one partly damaged hand. Major Stratton had provided the mares like Melissa said he would and on the odd occasion that Ryan had met him he'd been friendly and inquired about Ryan's new venture with the stud farm. Ryan had accepted that perhaps he and Melissa could never be more than friends because of their different backgrounds.

Ryan had hoped to see Janet during his latest visit to the saloon and had been disappointed to learn that she had left town. He had been thinking about making a move after the next beer so that he could check on the new foal when he sensed that the man across the other side of the bar was staring at him. The man looked as though he might have been living rough; his hair was shoulder length, greasy and unkempt as was his shaggy beard. Ryan held the man's stare for a moment and then turned away feeling that the man was probably just lost in his thoughts. Ryan took a final gulp of his beer and told the barman he was going to look in on the foal he had been telling him about.

As Ryan turned to walk away from the bar the bearded man was approaching him, but stopped by the bar and called out.

'Are you running away, Buchanan?'

Ryan studied the man's face now that he was closer. There was something familiar about him, but Ryan couldn't decide what it was. Ryan was in no doubt that the man was looking for trouble.

'What's your problem, stranger, and how come you know my name?'

'My father would still be alive if it wasn't for you and we've got some unfinished business. You do remember Karl Kruger, don't you?'

'Mark?' Ryan questioned, 'I didn't recognize you. I didn't have anything to do with your pa's death.'

'It was me who fired those shots, but they were meant for you. Pa told me to make sure that you didn't muscle in on Melissa.'

'So that's why you didn't turn up at your pa's funeral – because of your guilt.'

Kruger showed his anger at the accusation and dropped his hand near his pistol and Ryan followed suit, but he still hoped that he could calm Kruger down when he said, 'Why don't you just move on, Mark. What's done is done. Melissa was just a friend and she isn't ever coming back here.'

'You're lying. I saw her today at the Stratton ranch, but she didn't see me. She led me on before my pa died and

Major Stratton would have been happy if we had got together. We would have done if you hadn't have messed things up.'

Beads of sweat had formed on Kruger's face as he reached for his pistol, but he was clumsy and slow. He hadn't heard the news about Ryan's injuries or noticed his damaged hands or that he was wearing a left handed holster. Perhaps it was the fear of Ryan's reputation or the effects of the drink that allowed Ryan to beat Kruger to the draw and fire off a shot while Kruger was about to pull the trigger. Kruger fell to the saloon floor with a thud, a bullet embedded in his heart, and he began making an agonized groaning sound as he gasped for breath.

Mark Kruger was dead by the time the doc and the marshal arrived and the doc said it looked as though he might have had a heart attack, but he would have died from the gunshot wound. Marshal Clancy was as surprised as Ryan at the reappearance of Kruger after the rumours had emerged that he had been dismissed from the military.

The marshal took details of what had happened and then told Ryan that now the mystery shooting had been solved he really could get on with his life. The marshal's words should have brought some comfort to him, but they didn't because he could never forget that he might have killed Paul Bryce. He had never really believed that he had been with Melissa that night like she claimed. If he ever saw her again he would demand that she told him the truth and not just tease him about it like she had done before. He'd confessed to the marshal about his doubts, but the lawman had his own ideas about Paul Bryce's death; the marshal still had a hunch that Karl Kruger had been involved in Bryce's death, but he didn't know in what way.

TWENTY-FOUR

Ryan looked on as the roan foal suckled on the mare that was the pride of his breeding stock along with the stallion that had sired her. He was proud that he had built up the most prestigious stud farm in the territory and had sold horses far and wide, including the East. The army contract he had won during the early years had helped him to bring in new stock, but he also had his business partner to thank as well.

It is nearly ten years since Ryan shot and killed Mark Kruger in self defence on the day after Melissa had returned home to the Stratton Ranch. She came to see Ryan shortly after and told him that she planned to stay and live with her grandfather. They spent a lot of time together because of their shared interests in horses and her grandfather allowed her to invest in Ryan's stud farm. Major Stratton eventually accepted that Melissa and Ryan would never be just friends, but he did get his granddaughter to wait until after her twenty-first birthday before she married Ryan.

The carrying of arms is no longer permitted in most

towns, but Ryan still practises up at the canyon, although he has never managed to acquire the same skill he had before his right hand was damaged in the fire. He often recalls how lucky he'd been to get the better of Mark Kruger and not be the one to end up on the saloon floor.

Ryan plans to show his son Tom the gun he was given on his own eighteenth birthday when he is older, but he expects he will be amused by how dated it will look.

Melissa still teases him about the night that Bryce was killed and she claimed that Ryan was with her, but he also has a little secret that he hasn't told her. It was just over five years ago when a familiar name was mentioned to him. The name was Rob Slaney and he was one of the two ranch-hands who had left the day after they had claimed Ryan had killed Bryce. Marshal Clancy had arrested Slaney for assaulting a saloon girl when he was in a drunken stupor. The marshal had recognized Slaney and when he questioned him he claimed that Karl Kruger had paid him and his buddy Johansen to blame Ryan for the killing. Kruger had discovered that his son Mark had killed Bryce after they had argued when Melissa's party had ended and Karl Kruger was determined to pin it on Ryan.

The ranch that Major Stratton had longed to see stretch from the Deal Mountain range to the Mersey River did become a reality. The land belongs to Ryan and Melissa, who inherited the Stratton ranch when her grandfather died two years after she and Ryan were married. Melissa and Ryan prefer to live in the house they had built on the stud farm and appointed a manager to run the main ranch.

So Major Stratton never got to realize his ambition of owning the Buchanan land and Ryan never did break the promise he silently made to his ma on the day she was buried.